The Elephant

The Elephant

SLAWOMIR MROZEK

Translated from the Polish by Konrad Syrop

Illustrated by Daniel Mroz

GROVE PRESS, INC., NEW YORK

First published in Polish by Wydawnictwo Literackie, Krakow, 1958

First Evergreen Edition 1984
First Printing 1984

Library of Congress Cataloging in Publication Data

Mrożek, Sławomir.
    The elephant.
    Translation of: Słoń.
    I. Title.
PG7172.R65A27 1984   891.8'537   84-48113
                ISBN 0-394-62053-4 (pbk.)

A number of these stories have appeared in *Evergreen Review, Glamour, Harper's Bazaar, Harper's Magazine, Mademoiselle, Playboy,* and *The New York Times Magazine.*

Printed in the United States of America

GROVE PRESS, INC., 196 West Houston Street,
New York, N.Y., 10014

5   4   3   2   1

CONTENTS

CONTENTS

I

FROM THE DARKNESS

In this remote village of ours we are in the grip of terrible ignorance and superstition. Here I am, wanting to go outside to relieve myself, but at this moment hordes of bats are flying about, like leaves blown by an October wind, their wings knocking against the window panes, and I am afraid that one of them will get into my hair and I will never be able to get it out. So I am sitting here, comrades, instead of going out, repressing my need, and writing this report for you.

Well, as far as the purchase of grain is concerned, this has been falling ever since the devil appeared at the mill and took off his cap in an elegant greeting. His cap was in three colours: red, white and blue, and on it was embroidered *Tour de la Paix*. The peasants have been avoiding the mill, and the manager and his wife were driven by worry to drink until one day he splashed her with vodka and set her on fire. Then he left for the People's University, where he is going to read Marxism so that, as he says, he has something to put against those irrational elements.

And the manager's wife died in the flames and we have one more ghost.

I have to tell you that at night something howls here; howls so terribly that your heart almost stops beating. Some say that it is the spirit of poor Karas, who never had a bean, cursing the rich kulaks; others say that it is wealthy Krywon, complaining after death about the compulsory deliveries. A proper class war.

My cabin stands on the edge of the forest, alone. The night is black, the forest is black and my thoughts are like ravens. One day my neighbour, Jusienga, was sitting on a tree stump by the forest, reading *Horizons of Technology*, when something got at him from the back so that for three days he never stopped staring vacantly.

We need your advice, comrades, because we are alone here, miles from anywhere, surrounded only by distance and graves.

A forester has told me that at full moon in the clearings heads without bodies roll about, chase each other, knock at each other's cold foreheads as if they wanted something, but come dawn they all disappear and there are only trees left to murmur, not too loudly because they are afraid. Oh my God, nothing will make me go outside, not even the greatest need.

And it is the same with everything. You talk about Europe, comrades, but here. . . . No sooner do we pour our milk into jugs than hunchback dwarfs appear from somewhere and spit into it.

One night old Mrs. Glus woke up swimming in sweat. She looked at her eiderdown and what did she see? The small credit, that had been given to us before the elections (so that we could build a bridge here) and died suddenly without Extreme Unction, that credit was sitting on her eiderdown, all green and choking with laughter. The old woman started to scream but nobody came to see what was the matter. Can one be sure who is screaming and from what ideological position?

And at the spot where we were to have the bridge an artist got drowned. He was only two years old, but already a genius. Had he grown up he would have understood and described everything. But now all he can do is to fly about and fluoresce.

Of course, all those happenings have changed our psychology. People believe in sorcery and superstition. Only yesterday they found a skeleton behind Mocza's barn. The priest says that it is a political skeleton. They believe in ghosts and things, and even in witches. True, we have one woman who takes milk away from the cows and gives them fever, but we want to get her to join the Party and in this way deprive the enemies of progress of at least one argument.

How those bats flap their wings. Christ! how they fly and squeak "pee pee" and again "pee pee". There is nothing like those big houses where everything must be inside and there is no need to go into the bushes.

But there are even worse things than that. As I am writing this the door has opened and a pig's snout has appeared. It is looking at me very queerly, it is staring at me . . .

Have I not told you that things are different here?

2

BIRTHDAY

I paid my first call on the lawyer and his wife. Their drawing-room was in semi-darkness. Daylight was barely seeping through the curtains and through a jungle of asparagus fern. I found the lady of the house wearing a frock with a pattern of large, exotic butterflies. She was sitting in an easy chair that was draped in a white linen loose cover. From the dusk above my head a spider of a chandelier was peering at me, ringing softly with its crystal pendants whenever a heavy vehicle passed by. Only when my eyes got accustomed to the poor light did I notice in the far corner of the room, under a palm tree, some sort of a play-pen of the kind used by toddlers, only this one was much taller. Behind the wooden bars a man was sitting on a stool. He was doing embroidery.

As the hostess neither introduced us nor did she pay any attention to him, I felt it would have been tactless to make any enquiries and I pretended not to see him, but I was somewhat embarrassed. Custom prescribes that a visit of that nature should last a certain time; when this had elapsed I rose to go. On my way out I cast a curious glance at the play-pen but all I could see was the profile of a head bent over the embroidery. The hostess saw me to the door and, before we parted, invited me to her husband's birthday party the following Saturday.

As a stranger to the little town I was not familiar with its peculiarities, among which I counted what I had just seen in the lawyer's drawing-room. I assumed, however, that my next visit would bring a solution of the mystery.

On the appointed day I dressed carefully and made for the lawyer's villa. I could see it from a distance, not only because it was the most imposing house in the town, but, on this occasion, it was brightly illuminated, its lights reflected in the bakelite-black river which was flowing near by. A firework broke in the sky above the town hall—that was the local militia station joining in the celebrations of the lawyer's birthday in which the whole population of the town was taking part.

The gate was ajar. Through the half-open front door light was falling on the path. I entered the drawing-room and was blinded by the blaze of the chandelier. The white loose covers had disappeared from the easy chairs. I noticed among those present the red face of the priest and the yellow faces of the chemist and his wife; the doctor and the chairman of the work co-operative were there, both with their wives, and the owner of a modest workshop which produced penholders for the Government. He, too, had his spouse with him. The lawyer came forward to greet me.

I offered my best wishes and handed over my present. His wife, who was wearing a magnificent gown, invited me to sit down. At first I could not very well look round, but when I joined in the conversation I started to glance unobtrusively in the direction of the corner of the room. Yes, I was not mistaken. Under the palm tree was the pen, and inside it the man. He was somewhat better dressed than the last time I saw him and he seemed to be dozing with his head resting in his hands. As far as politeness permitted I kept on watching him out of the corner of my eye, but the other guests, all of them frequent visitors to the house, paid not the slightest attention to him and were engrossed in their loud and gay conversation, as becomes a birthday party. It seemed to me that the man, feeling my eyes on him, woke up for a moment, but immediately went back to sleep with complete indifference.

For some time, while joining in the laughter and discussion, pulling the leg of the chemist and exchanging thoughts with the priest, I tried in vain to solve the riddle. Suddenly the double doors were thrown open and the servants brought in a table resplendent with silver and food and drink. The host's children made their appearance, and amid the general animation caused by the arrival of the supper we all sat down at the table. A few toasts added to the gaiety of the company, the hubbub of voices grew louder. Then, through the tinkling of glasses, the din of knives and forks, the silvery laughter of women and the throaty jokes of men, I could hear singing. Yes, it was the man in the pen. To the soft accompaniment of a balalaika came the nostalgic melody of "Volga, Volga . . ." The company greeted the song with utter indifference as if it were a canary singing.

Next came "Black Eyes", followed by a gayer song. Dessert was being served and soon the table was enveloped in a cloud of cigarette smoke. I noticed that the host's children, with the permission of their mother, took a bottle of cherry brandy from the table and poured some of it through the wooden bars into a glass which they had given to the man. He put his balalaika aside, drank the brandy, and then resumed his singing.

The priest started a discussion with me on the subject of Darwin's theory of evolution, so I could not watch the man in the pen with any great attention. "There are those," argued the priest, "who claim that man is a descendant of the monkey. One thing is certain: those who say so are themselves descendants of apes." I was beginning to feel the effect of all the drinks I had had, but I noticed that the man in the pen himself was under the influence of alcohol.

13

My host caught the direction of my gaze. "Do you know who that is?" he asked with a laugh. "It was an idea of my wife's. She wouldn't have a canary or anything like that in her drawing-room. It's common, she says. So I got her a live progressive. Don't be afraid of him. He's been tamed."

The other guests, amused, were staring at the man with the balalaika. The lawyer continued his explanation.

"He's local. For a few years he was wild and even caused some damage, but recently he became tame, so we keep him in the house. He embroiders, plays the balalaika and sings, but sometimes he looks as if he were longing for something."

"Perhaps he's longing for freedom, or action . . ." I suggested timidly. "After all he's a progressive."

"Come, now. He's never had it so good," objected the lawyer. "He has a roof over his head and assured food, peace, no trouble whatsoever. We've trained him to eat out of our hands—you saw for yourself. He isn't dangerous. We let him out for the National Day celebrations and for the anniversary of the Revolution, so that he can get some exercise. But he always comes back. Anyhow, this is a small town; there's nowhere for him to hide."

While the lawyer was imparting this information to me, the subject of the conversation was gazing around. His brow furrowed. Under his stare the priest's hand, which was transporting a piece of Emmenthaler to his mouth, was suddenly arrested in mid-air. Conversation stopped. In the silence we heard the rattle of a spoon which fell from the chairman's fingers. Even the lawyer became serious. The man, fixing his eyes on the banqueting table, grasped the balalaika and began to sing: "To the barricades, workers advance . . ."

There was general feeling of relief. The priest swallowed his Emmenthaler and everybody listened to the song with interest. "First class!" shouted the lawyer, laughing and slapping his thighs. The chemist was bent in two with merriment. Only the hostess was displeased.

"Darling," she said to her husband, "it's late. Don't you think the children should go to bed? And he, he should be covered with his blanket, so that he won't sing any more tonight."

"Right," said the lawyer, "let the progressive get some sleep."

Late that night, when I was among the last guests to go, I passed the pen. It was covered with a velvet bedspread embroidered in mauve flowers. It seemed to me that from underneath it I could hear the soft strains of the balalaika and some singing. I thought I heard the words:

"Forward, forward . . ."

3

THE ELEPHANT

The director of the Zoological Gardens has shown himself to be an upstart. He regarded his animals simply as stepping stones on the road of his own career. He was indifferent to the educational importance of his establishment. In his Zoo the giraffe had a short neck, the badger had no burrow and the whistlers, having lost all interest, whistled rarely and with some reluctance. These shortcomings should not have been allowed, especially as the Zoo was often visited by parties of schoolchildren.

The Zoo was in a provincial town, and it was short of some of the most important animals, among them the elephant. Three thousand rabbits were a poor substitute for the noble giant. However, as our country developed, the gaps were being filled in a well-planned manner. On the occasion of the anniversary of the liberation, on 22nd July, the Zoo was notified that it had at long last been allocated an elephant. All the staff, who were devoted to their work, rejoiced at this news. All the greater was their surprise when they learnt that the director had sent a letter to Warsaw, renouncing the allocation and putting forward a plan for obtaining an elephant by more economic means.

"I, and all the staff," he had written, "are fully aware how heavy a burden falls upon the shoulders of Polish miners and foundry men because of the elephant. Desirous of reducing our costs, I suggest that the elephant mentioned in your communication should be replaced by one of our own procurement. We can make an elephant out of rubber, of the correct size, fill it with air and place it behind railings. It will be carefully painted the correct colour and even on close inspection will be indistinguishable from the real animal. It is well known that the elephant is a sluggish animal and it does not run and jump about. In the notice on the railings we can state that this particular elephant is exceptionally sluggish. The money saved in this way can be turned to the purchase of a jet plane or the conservation of some church monument.

"Kindly note that both the idea and its execution are my modest contribution to the common task and struggle.

"I am, etc."

This communication must have reached a soulless official, who regarded his duties in a purely bureaucratic manner and did not examine the heart of the matter but, following only the directive about reduction of expenditure, accepted the director's plan. On hearing the Ministry's approval, the director issued instructions for the making of the rubber elephant.

The carcase was to have been filled with air by two keepers blowing into it from opposite ends. To keep the operation secret the work was to be completed during the night because the people of the town, having heard that an elephant was joining the Zoo, were anxious to see it. The director insisted on haste also because he expected a bonus, should his idea turn out to be a success.

The two keepers locked themselves in a shed normally housing a workshop, and began to blow. After two hours of hard blowing they discovered that the rubber skin had risen only a few inches above the floor and its bulge in no way resembled an elephant. The night progressed. Outside, human voices were stilled and only the cry of the jackass interrupted the silence. Exhausted, the keepers stopped blowing and made sure that the air already inside the elephant should not escape. They were not young and were unaccustomed to this kind of work.

"If we go on at this rate," said one of them, "we shan't finish before the morning. And what am I to tell my Missus? She'll never believe me if I say that I spent the night blowing up an elephant."

"Quite right," agreed the second keeper. "Blowing up an elephant is not an everyday job. And it's all because our director is a leftist."

They resumed their blowing, but after another half-an-hour they felt too tired to continue. The bulge on the floor was larger but still nothing like the shape of an elephant.

"It's getting harder all the time," said the first keeper.

"It's an uphill job, all right," agreed the second. "Let's have a little rest."

While they were resting, one of them noticed a gas pipe ending in a valve. Could they not fill the elephant with gas? He suggested it to his mate.

They decided to try. They connected the elephant to the gas pipe, turned the valve, and to their joy in a few minutes there was a full-sized beast standing in the shed. It looked real: the enormous body, legs like columns, huge ears and the inevitable trunk. Driven by ambition the director had made sure of having in his Zoo a very large elephant indeed.

"First class," declared the keeper who had the idea of using gas. "Now we can go home."

In the morning the elephant was moved to a special run in a central position, next to the monkey cage. Placed in front of a large real rock it looked fierce and magnificent. A big notice proclaimed: "Particularly sluggish. Hardly moves."

Among the first visitors that morning was a party of children

from the local school. The teacher in charge of them was planning to give them an object-lesson about the elephant. He halted the group in front of the animal and began:

"The elephant is a herbivorous mammal. By means of its trunk it pulls out young trees and eats their leaves."

The children were looking at the elephant with enraptured admiration. They were waiting for it to pull out a young tree, but the beast stood still behind its railings.

". . . The elephant is a direct descendant of the now extinct mammoth. It's not surprising, therefore, that it's the largest living land animal."

The more conscientious pupils were making notes.

". . . Only the whale is heavier than the elephant, but then the whale lives in the sea. We can safely say that on land the elephant reigns supreme."

A slight breeze moved the branches of the trees in the Zoo.

". . . The weight of a fully grown elephant is between nine and thirteen thousand pounds."

At that moment the elephant shuddered and rose in the air. For a few seconds it swayed just above the ground but a gust of wind blew it upwards until its mighty silhouette was against the sky. For a short while people on the ground could still see the four circles of its feet, its bulging belly and the trunk, but soon, propelled by the wind, the elephant sailed above the fence and disappeared above the tree-tops. Astonished monkeys in the cage continued staring into the sky.

They found the elephant in the neighbouring botanical gardens. It had landed on a cactus and punctured its rubber hide.

The schoolchildren who had witnessed the scene in the Zoo soon started neglecting their studies and turned into hooligans. It is reported that they drink liquor and break windows. And they no longer believe in elephants.

4

A SILENT HERO

One afternoon, when I looked out of the window, I saw a funeral moving down the street. A simple coffin on an austere hearse drawn only by one horse. Behind the hearse walked the widow, clad in black, and three other people, probably relatives or friends of the deceased.

The modest cortège would not have attracted my attention were it not for the fact that the coffin was covered with a red banner bearing the inscription THREE CHEERS.

Intrigued, I left my flat and joined the procession. Soon we reached the cemetery. The deceased was buried in a far corner among a group of birch trees. I kept myself in the background during the burial rites, but afterwards I approached the widow to offer my condolences and to enquire about the identity of the deceased.

I learnt that he had been a civil servant. Moved by my interest in her late husband, the widow volunteered some information about his last days. She complained that her husband had exhausted himself by undertaking unusual voluntary work: he spent all his free time writing memoranda and letters describing new methods of propaganda. Just before his death his sole aim seemed to be to translate propaganda slogans into action.

My curiosity was aroused and I asked to be allowed to see some of her husband's writings. She agreed readily and gave me two sheets of yellowing paper, covered with a precise, somewhat old-fashioned handwriting. That is how I came to read his memorandum.

"Let us consider flies, for instance," was the opening sentence. "After dinner I often watch flies circling round the lamp and this stimulates various thoughts in my head. Would it not be wonderful, I think, if flies could share in our social consciousness. Then, if you caught one of them, pulled off its wings, dipped it in ink and let it loose on a clean sheet of paper, it would move about, writing SUPPORT THE AIR FORCE or another slogan."

The spiritual profile of the deceased became clearer to me as I read on. He must have been a sincere man, deeply concerned with the idea of placing slogans and banners whenever and wherever possible. Among his most original ideas was the sowing of special clover.

"Through the co-operation of artists and biologists," he wrote, "it should be possible to breed a special kind of clover. At present this plant has flowers of one colour, but if the seed were suitably prepared, the flowers could grow in the likeness of one of the leaders or a hero of labour. Just imagine a whole field of clover at flowering time! Of course, one would have to guard against mistakes. It would be most unfortunate if, through the mixing up of seeds, a leader's face, which is normally devoid of moustache and spectacles, should appear in flower form with both. The only remedy would be to mow the whole field and sow again."

The ideas of the old man were more and more intriguing. After having read his memorandum I came to the conclusion that the slogan THREE CHEERS had been placed on his coffin at his own express wish. In this way, even during his last journey, the selfless inventor and fanatical propagandist wished to demonstrate his enthusiasm.

I was curious to discover the exact circumstances of his death and made enquiries. It was no surprise to be told that he had fallen victim of his own eagerness. On the occasion of the National Day he took off all his clothes and painted his body in seven vertical stripes of various colours. Then he went out on his balcony, climbed on the balustrade and tried to do what is known to some physical exercise enthusiasts as "the crab"—a back-bend in which the arched body rests on the subject's hands and feet. In this way he wished to create a living picture of a rainbow—the symbol of hope. Alas, the balcony was thirty feet above ground level.

I went to the cemetery to have another look at his last resting place. Though I searched for a long time, I could not find the group of birches among which he had been buried. In the end I decided to follow a passing band returning from a tattoo. It was playing a gay march.

5

CHILDREN

That winter there was plenty of snow.

In the square children were making a snowman.

The square was vast. Many people passed through it every day and the windows of many offices kept it under constant observation. The square did not mind, it just continued to stretch into the distance. In the very centre of it the children, laughing and shouting, were engaged in the making of a ridiculous figure.

First they rolled a large ball. That was the trunk. Next came a smaller ball—the shoulders. An even smaller ball followed—the head. Tiny pieces of coal made a row of suitable buttons running from top to bottom. The nose consisted of a carrot. In other words it was a perfectly ordinary snowman, not unlike the thousands of similar figures which, the snow permitting, spring up across the country every year.

All this gave the children a great deal of fun. They were very happy.

Many passers-by stopped to admire the snowman and went on their way. Government offices continued to work as if nothing had happened.

The children's father was glad that they should be getting exercise in the fresh air, acquiring rosy cheeks and healthy appetites.

In the evening, when they were all at home, someone

knocked at the door. It was the newsagent who had a kiosk in the square. He apologised profusely for disturbing the family so late and for troubling them, but he felt it his duty to have a few words with the father. Of course, he knew the children were still small, but that made it all the more important to keep an eye on them, in their own interest. He would not have dared to come were it not for his concern for the little ones. One could say his visit had an educational purpose. It was about the snowman's nose the children had made out of a carrot. It was a red nose. Now, he, the newsagent, also had a red nose. Frostbite, not drink, you know. Surely there could be no earthly reason for making a public allusion to the colour of his nose. He would be grateful if this did not happen again. He really had the upbringing of the children at heart.

The father was worried by this speech. Of course children could not be allowed to ridicule people, even those with red noses. They were probably still too young to understand. He called them, and, pointing at the newsagent, asked severely: "Is it true that, with this gentleman in mind, you gave your snowman a red nose?"

The children were genuinely surprised. At first they did not see the point of the question. When they did, they answered that the thought had never crossed their minds.

Just in case, they were told to go to bed without supper.

The newsagent was grateful and made for the door. There he met face to face with the Chairman of the Co-operative. The father was delighted to greet such a distinguished person in his house.

On seeing the children, the Chairman chided: "Ah, here are your brats. You must keep them under control, you know. Small, but already impertinent. What do you think I saw from the window of my office this afternoon? If you please, they were making a snowman."

"If it's about its nose . . ."

"Nose, fiddlesticks! Just imagine, first they made one ball of snow, then another and yet another. And then what do you think? They put one ball on top of the other and the third on top of both of them. Isn't it exasperating?"

The father did not understand and the Chairman went on angrily: "You don't see! But it's crystal clear what they meant. They wanted to say that in our Co-operative one thief sits on top of another. And that's libel. Even when one writes such things to the papers one has to produce some proof, and all the more so when one makes a public demonstration in the square."

However, the Chairman was a considerate, tolerant man. He would make allowances for youth and thoughtlessness. He would not insist on a public apology. But it must not happen again.

Asked if, when putting one snowball on top of the other, they wished to convey that in the Co-operative one thief was sitting on top of another, the children replied in the negative and burst into tears. Just in case, however, they were ordered to stand in a corner.

That was not the end of the day. Sleigh bells could be heard outside and soon two men were at the door. One of them was a fat stranger in a sheepskin coat, the other—the President of the local National Council himself.

"It's about your children," they announced in unison from the door.

These calls were becoming a matter of routine. Both men were offered chairs. The President looked askance at the stranger, wondering who he might be, and decided to speak first.

"I'm astonished that you should tolerate subversive activities in your own family. But perhaps you are politically ignorant? If so, you'd better admit it right away."

The father did not understand why he should be politically ignorant.

"One can see it at a glance by your children's behaviour. Who makes fun of the People's authority? Your children do. They made a snowman outside the window of my study."

"Oh, I understand," whispered the father, "you mean that one thief . . ."

"Thief, my foot. But do you know the meaning of the snowman outside the window of the President of the National Council? I know very well what people are saying about me. Why don't your brats make a snowman outside Adenauer's window, for instance? Well, why not? You don't answer. That silence speaks volumes. You'll have to take the consequences."

On hearing the word "consequences" the fat stranger rose and furtively tiptoed out of the room. Outside, the sleigh bells tinkled and faded into the distance.

"Yes, my dear sir," the President said, "you'd better reflect on all these implications. And one more thing. It's entirely my private affair that I walk about my house with my fly undone and your children have no right to make fun of it. Those buttons on the snowman, from top to bottom, that's ambiguous. And I'll tell you something: if I like, I can walk about my house without my trousers and it's none of your children's business. You'd better remember that."

The accused summoned his children from the corner and demanded that they confess. When making the snowman had they had the President in mind and, by adorning the figure with buttons from top to bottom had they made an additional joke, in very bad taste, alluding to the fact that the President walks about his house with his fly undone?

With tears in their eyes the children assured him that they had made the snowman just for fun, without any ulterior motive. Just in case, however, apart from being deprived of their supper and sent to the corner, they were now made to kneel on the hard floor.

That night several more people knocked at the door but they obtained no reply.

The following morning I was passing a little garden and I saw the children there. The square having been declared out of bounds the children were discussing how best to occupy themselves in the confined space.

"Let's make a snowman," said one.

"An ordinary snowman is no fun," said another.

"Let's make the newsagent. We'll give him a red nose, because he drinks. He said so himself last night," said the third.

"And I want to make the Co-op."

"And I want to make the President, silly fool. And we'll give him buttons because he walks with his fly undone."

There was an argument but in the end the children agreed; they would make all of them in turn.

They started working with gusto.

6

THE TRIAL

At long last the aim has been achieved and a tremendous amount of work and effort has borne fruit. All the authors have been put into uniform and awarded suitable ranks and distinctions. In this way chaos, lack of criteria, unhealthy artistic tendencies and the obscurity and ambiguity of art have been removed once and for all.

The design of the uniforms had been worked out centrally; the division into districts and formations, as well as the system of ranks to be awarded to individual members, were the result of long preparatory work in the Supreme Council of the Writers' Association. From then on every member had to wear a uniform consisting of wide mauve trousers with piping of a different colour, green jacket, belt and peaked hat. Thus the basic uniform was simple, but it allowed for a great variety of rank. Members of the Supreme Council wore two-peaked hats with gold braid, but members of regional councils were entitled only to silver braid. Chairmen wore swords, vice-chairmen stilettos.

All the writers were assigned to appropriate formations according to their *genre*. Two regiments of poets were set up, three divisions of practitioners in prose and one firing squad composed of various elements. The greatest changes took place among the literary critics; some of them were banished to the salt mines and the remainder incorporated in the gendarmerie.

Everybody was given a rank within a scale ranging from Private to Marshal. The deciding factors were the number of words published by each author during his lifetime, the angle of his ideological spine in relation to the floor, his age and his position in local or national government. Flashes of different colours distinguished the various ranks.

The advantages of this new order were self-evident. First of all it was clear to everybody what he should think of any author; a writer-general could not possibly write a bad novel and, obviously, the best novels had to come from the pen of a writer-marshal. A writer-colonel might make mistakes but, even so, he must be much more talented than a writer-major.

The work of editorial offices was greatly simplified; it was easy to calculate quickly and accurately how much more suitable for publication was the work of a writer-brigadier than that of a writer-lieutenant. In the same way the question of fees was settled automatically.

It became impossible for a critic-writer-captain to commit to paper any adverse views on the work of anyone holding the rank of writer-major or above and only a critic-writer-general could find fault with something coming from the pen of a writer-colonel.

The advantages of the new order were not confined to the literary profession. Before the reform processions and public ceremonies were marred by the dreary appearance of the writers who compared unfavourably with the sportsmen. Now the writers' detachment presented a gay and colourful spectacle. The glitter of gold and silver braid, the multi-coloured flashes and piping, the peaked hats, all this appealed to the crowd and led to a great increase in the popularity of the writers among the people.

It must be admitted that certain difficulties were encountered in connection with the classification of one eccentric writer.

Though he wrote prose his works were too short to be described as novels and too long for short stories. Moreover, rumour had it that his prose had a poetic quality and a satirical bent, and that he wrote articles which were indistinguishable from stories and also bore the characteristics of critical essays. It was thought improper to assign this writer either to a prose or to a poetry detachment and it was clearly impracticable to create a special formation for one man only. There were suggestions that he would be expelled, but in the end a compromise was reached; he was given orange-coloured trousers, the rank of a private and was left to his own devices. The whole country could thus see that he was really a blot on the profession. Had he been expelled this would not have been without precedent. At an earlier stage several writers who, because of their build, did not look well in uniform had been removed from the association.

Within a short time the country discovered that leaving the eccentric in the ranks of writers had been a serious mistake. It was he who was the cause of a scandalous affair which undermined the beautifully simple principles of authority.

One day a well-known and respected writer-general was taking a walk along a boulevard in the capital city. Approaching him from the opposite direction was the eccentric writer-private in orange trousers. The writer-general threw him a contemptuous glance and waited for the private's salute. Suddenly he noticed on the private's hat the insignia of the highest rank, a small red beetle, which only writer-marshals were entitled to wear. Respect for authority was so deeply embedded in the writer-general that, without pausing to consider the unusual nature of his discovery, he immediately adopted a most respectful attitude and saluted first. The astonished writer-private returned the salute, and as his hand went up to his hat, the large ladybird that had been sitting there opened its wings and flew away. Gripped by anger because of this humiliation, the writer-general immediately summoned a patrolling critic who took away the private's fountain-pen and escorted him to the guard-room in the House of Literature.

The trial took place in the marble hall of the Palace of the Arts. Judges and other dignitaries sat behind a large mahogany table, their glistening epaulettes and golden insignia reflected in the dark, mirror-like surface.

The eccentric writer-private was accused of illegally wearing insignia to which he was not entitled by his rank. However, luck was on his side. On the eve of the trial, during a meeting of the Council for Culture, strong criticism had been voiced of the soulless attitude to the artist and of the way art was being administered. Echoes of this debate could be heard the following day when the critic-writer-marshal himself rose to speak during the trial.

"We must on no account," he proclaimed, "adopt a bureaucratic attitude to this case. Our task is to get to the very bottom of this affair. Without doubt the case we are trying here today concerns the violation of those rules which, in spite of some mistakes, have led to an unprecedented flowering of our literature. The question we must ask, however, is this: 'Is the accused a conscious and active criminal?' We must probe deeply in search of the answer, we must expose not only the effects of this act but also its causes. Let's consider first of all who brought the accused to his present sorry condition. Who has depraved him, who has exploited his initial lack of social consciousness? What sort of creative atmosphere could have led to this crisis? To whom must we mete out punishment so as to prevent similar trials in the future?

"No, comrades. It's not the accused who is mainly responsible. He was only a tool in the hands of the ladybird. There can be no doubt whatsoever that the ladybird, motivated by

hatred of our new hierarchy, incensed by the achievements of our system of absolutely precise criteria and by the perfect organisation of our association . . . the ladybird with treacherous deliberation alighted on the hat of the accused and imitated a marshal's insignia. It's the ladybird who has tried to undermine our hierarchy. Let's punish the hand and not the blind tool."

The speech was greeted as a profound exploration of the very roots of evil. The writer-private was rehabilitated and a proper indictment was prepared against the ladybird.

A platoon of critics found the ladybird in a garden, sitting on a lilac leaf and plotting. When the ladybird realised that it had been unmasked, it offered no resistance.

The new trial took place in the same marble hall. All those present were straining their eyes to see the little red spot on the shiny table. Under a glass saucer, which prevented its escape, the ladybird sat still and unrepentant in its crime, preserving a disdainful silence to the very end.

The execution took place at dawn the following morning. Four thick and well-bound volumes of the latest novel by the writer-marshal of literature were the chosen instrument. They were dropped one by one from the height of four feet. It is reported that the condemned did not suffer long.

When the writer-private in orange trousers heard about the verdict, he cried and asked that the ladybird be set free in a garden. This brought him under suspicion once more of having been at least an accomplice in this crime; his attachment to the ladybird was thought to be highly suggestive.

7

THE SWAN

In the park was a lake. On the lake lived a swan. It was the chief attraction of the park. One day the swan disappeared. It had been stolen by hooligans.

The department of Municipal Gardens procured a new swan. A special guard was appointed to protect the bird from its predecessor's fate.

The post was given to a little old man who had been lonely for years. When he took up his job evenings were already beginning to turn chilly. The park was deserted. While patrolling the lake the old man kept an eye on the swan, but sometimes he allowed himself a glance at the stars. He was cold. It would be lovely, he thought, to look in at the small restaurant near the park. He started in that direction but remembered the swan. Someone might steal the bird while he was away. He would lose his job. The idea had to be given up.

But the bitter cold kept on nagging at him, increasing his loneliness. In the end he decided to go to the restaurant and take the swan with him. Even should someone come to the park, while they were away, to breathe in the beauty of nature he would not notice the absence of the swan immediately. It was a starlit, but moonless, night and they would be back shortly.

They went.

In the restaurant they were greeted by a comforting wave of warm air carrying delicious smells of frying food. The old man put the swan on a chair at the opposite side of the table and sat down. In this way he could watch his charge while consuming a modest meal. To warm himself he also ordered a small glass of vodka.

When he was eating a dish of mutton, and enjoying it hugely, he noticed that the swan was gazing at him unhappily. The old man felt sorry for the bird. Under the swan's reproachful eyes he lost all desire for food. Then he had an idea. He called the waiter and ordered a roll and some hot beer with sugar. Dipping the roll in the beer he fed the swan and the bird quickly regained its good humour. After the meal, satisfied and refreshed, they both returned to their posts.

The next evening was even colder. On that occasion the stars seemed uncommonly bright and the old guard felt each of them as an ice-cold nail driven into his warm but lonely heart. However, he resisted the temptation to visit the restaurant once more.

In the centre of the lake the swan appeared, its white feathers glowing gently in the starlight.

The thought of any living creature being in contact with water on that bitterly cold evening made the old man shiver. Poor swan, he deserved a better fate. The guard was sure that the bird would welcome some warmth and food.

So he took the swan under his arm and carried it to the restaurant.

Another cold evening came and filled the old man with gloom. This time he was determined not to visit the restaurant because, the night before, after their return, the swan had danced and sang in a most peculiar fashion.

So he sat by the edge of the lake in the empty cold park and observed the sky. Suddenly he felt that someone was tugging at his trousers. It was the swan asking for something. They went.

A month later both the guard and the swan were dismissed by the authorities. The swan had been observed reeling about in the water, in broad daylight too. A mother, who had brought her small children to the park to see the swan, complained to the authorities, of course purely out of consideration for the young.

Even in the most modest position its holder must have some moral principles.

8

TINY

There was once a theatrical company of dwarfs which appeared under the name of "Teeny Theatre". It was a reliable, permanent troupe which performed at least four times a week and bravely tackled all problems. Small wonder that, in due course, the Ministry of Culture raised it to the rank of a model Lilliputian theatre and gave it the official name of "The Central Teeny Theatre". This guaranteed excellent conditions to the company, and to join it became the ambition of every dwarf actor, be he amateur or professional. However, the troupe already had all the actors it needed, including some outstandingly gifted performers. Among its leading lights was a midget who was always entrusted with leading rôles because he was the smallest of them all. He earned good money and the critics always stressed his excellent technique. On one occasion he even reached such a degree of excellence in the part of Hamlet that though he was on the stage the spectators did not see him, so small, so exquisitely and perfectly small was he. Intellectually he was one of us, in appearance he belonged to Lilliput. The success of the theatre was largely due to him.

One day, when he was putting on make-up in his dressing-room before the first night of an historical play in which he naturally was to act the leading part of the king, he noticed that he could not see in the mirror the reflection of the golden

38

crown he was wearing on his head. Later, as he was going out into the corridor, he did not realise that the door was too low and the crown was knocked off his head and rolled away with a loud metallic clatter. He picked it up and went on the stage. After the first act, as he returned to his dressing-room, he instinctively lowered his head in the door. The building of the "Central Teeny" had been designed especially on the scale of the actors, the state subsidy paying for the marble and the artificial clay imported from as far as Novosibirsk for the construction of the theatre.

Performances of the historic play continued one after another and the diminutive actor got used to lowering his head on entering and leaving the dressing-room. On one occasion, however, he noticed the old theatre barber watching him intently. The barber was also a dwarf, but taller than the others and thus considered unsuitable for acting; this condemned him to work behind the scenes and filled his heart with hatred and envy. The barber's gaze was thoughtful and sinister. An unhappy feeling gripped the tiny actor and it would not leave him for a long time. In vain did he try to dismiss this feeling; it was there when he went to sleep and when he woke up. He tried to ignore it and to suppress the suspicion which started to develop in his mind. Time brought no relief. On the contrary. The day came when he had to bend in the door of his dressing-room even though he wore no headgear. In the corridor he passed the barber.

That day he decided to face the truth. Even the superficial measurements he made behind the drawn curtains of his elegant apartment left no room for doubt. He could cherish no more illusions. He was growing.

That night he sat almost paralysed in his easy chair, a glass of grog by his side, staring at the photograph of his father, also a dwarf. The next day he removed the heels from his shoes in the hope that his predicament was only temporary, that perhaps he would eventually shrink to his original size. For a time the removal of the heels did the trick. But one day, because of the presence of the barber, he left his dressing-room fully erect and nearly knocked himself out in the doorway. He could not help noticing the scorn on the face of the barber.

Why was he growing? Why should his hormones wake up from their sleep after all those years? In desperation his mind fastened on an idea. He remembered the frequent propaganda slogan: "Here people grow . . ." Ordinary people? Yes, but dwarfs? Just in case, he stopped listening to the radio, gave up reading newspapers and deliberately neglected his ideological education. He tried to persuade himself that he was an anti-social being, he even tried to overcome his natural disgust and became an apologist of imperialism, but all this was artificial and of no avail. His irrepressible class instinct, inherited from his pauper dwarf father, proved stronger. He threw himself into the other extreme, went on sprees in kindergartens and drank by the thimbleful in an attempt to drown his sorrow. Meanwhile time mercilessly but almost imperceptibly kept on adding to his size.

Did his colleagues know? On several occasions he caught the barber whispering with the actors in the wings. As soon as he approached the whispering gave way to an exchange of banal remarks. He watched his comrades' faces but could read nothing in them. In the street less and less frequently was he stopped by women asking: "Have you lost your mummy, boy?" On one occasion he heard for the first time in his life someone say to him: "Excuse me, sir." After that incident he hastily went home and threw himself on his divan. For a long time he lay motionless, staring at the ceiling, but finally he had to change his position because of the cramp in his legs which were hanging over the edge of the already too short divan.

In the end he could have no doubt about his colleagues at the theatre. They knew or they guessed the truth. He also noticed that the critics were no longer enthusiastic about his performances and even favourable mentions became rare. Or was it perhaps his excited imagination playing tricks on him, discovering everywhere derision or compassion? Fortunately there was no change in the attitude of the management. His success in the historical play was, after all, considerable, even if not as sweeping as in the part of Hamlet. Without hesitation he was given the leading part in the forthcoming production.

He suffered much during the rehearsals but somehow reached the first night without any special difficulty. Before the curtain rose he was sitting in his dressing-room, already made-up, facing the mirror but avoiding his own reflection. He was ready. On the summons of the call-boy he rose heavily; his head hit the ceiling light and broke it. He turned towards the open door and in the brightly lit corridor he saw practically the whole company standing in a semi-circle with the barber in the centre. Next to the barber was his chief rival, another leading actor, who hitherto had always been an inch or so taller than himself.

There was no way out; he had to give up acting. As he grew taller he tried various occupations. For a while he was an extra in crowd scenes at the children's theatre, later a messenger boy, a pointsman for the municipal tramways . . . From time to time, because he could not earn enough to support himself, he sold some of the possessions he had accumulated during his years of glory. And then he grew a little more and stayed like that, a man of medium height.

What did he feel? Did he suffer much? His name, covered by the dust of time, had long since disappeared from the hoardings. He took a clerk's job in the State Insurance Department.

One Saturday, several years later, trying to occupy his free evening, he found himself in a theatre watching a performance by a company of dwarf actors. Sucking mint sweets he laughed at the jokes on the stage, fairly amused, fairly interested. When it ended, comfortable in the knowledge that supper was awaiting him at home, he said to himself:

"Yes, those tiny ones are quite fun."

9

THE LION

The Emperor gave the sign. The iron grille, enclosing the entrance to the tunnel, rose and from the darkness came a crescendo of menacing roars. In the centre of the arena a group of Christians drew closer together. The spectators were on their feet. Excited chatter, cries of fear and the roar approaching like an avalanche. From the tunnel emerged the first lioness moving swiftly and silently. The spectacle had begun.

Armed with a long pole the keeper of the lions, Gaius, was checking if all the beasts had gone into the arena to take part in the terrible entertainment. He was about to give a sigh of relief when he noticed that one lion had stopped just short of the entrance and was calmly chewing a carrot. Gaius swore. One of his duties was to ensure that no beast remained idle. He approached the lion as far as safety and health regulations permitted and prodded the animal's rump with his pole. To his surprise the lion only turned his head and swung his tail. Gaius prodded again, harder this time.

"Oh, leave me alone," said the lion.

Gaius scratched his head. The lion had made it crystal clear that it did not wish to go into the arena. Gaius was a kind man but he was afraid that if the supervisor caught him neglecting his duties he would soon find himself among the victims in the arena.

43

On the other hand he did not feel like arguing with the lion. He tried persuasion.

"Perhaps you'll go out just for my sake?"

"I'm no fool," replied the lion and continued to eat his carrot.

Gaius lowered his voice.

"I'm not saying that you have to jump at one of those wretches and tear him to pieces. Just go and run about a little and roar. That'll give us an alibi."

The lion swung his tail.

"Man, I've told you that I'm no fool. They'll see me and remember me. Later nobody will believe that I didn't eat one of them."

The keeper sighed and asked with an accent of complaint: "And why don't you want to?"

The lion looked at him attentively.

"You've yourself used the word 'alibi'. Hasn't it occurred to you why all those patricians there don't run into the arena and themselves tear the Christians to pieces, but instead rely on us, the lions?"

"Oh, I don't know. They are mostly old men. Short of breath, you know. Asthma. . . ."

"Old men," purred the lion mockingly. "You know a lot about politics. They simply want to have an alibi."

"Why?"

"Because of the new truth that is gaining ground. One has always to watch what's new and growing. Has it never crossed your mind that the Christians could come to power?"

"They—to power?"

"Yes. One has got to be able to read between the lines. It looks to me as if Constantine the Great is likely to come to terms with them sooner or later. And then what? Investigations and rehabilitations. Then those up there in the amphitheatre will be able to say: 'It wasn't us, it was the lions.'"

"Really, I never thought of it that way."

"There you are. But never mind them. I want to save my own skin. When it comes to it there will be witnesses to say that all I did was to eat a carrot. Mind you, it's filthy stuff, this carrot."

"But all your comrades," said Gaius not without malice, "they are all gobbling up the Christians with great gusto."

"Stupid beasts. Short-sighted opportunists. No tactical sense at all. From darkest Africa——"

"I say," interrupted Gaius.

"Yes?"

"Should those Christians, you know . . ."

"What about them?"

"Should they come to power . . ."

"Well?"

"Will you then testify that I didn't force you to do anything?"

"*Salus Respublicae summa lex tibi esto*," said the lion sententiously and returned to his carrot.

10

THE PARABLE OF THE MIRACULOUS ESCAPE

I shall now tell you a tale that will warm your hearts and show you the inscrutable ways Divine providence takes to lead us to salvation. It's a tale of true events.

Before the war there lived in our city of Hamburg a man named Eric Kraus. He had a wife and four children. Unfortunately he kept bad company and under the influence of his colleagues he came to doubt the rightness and justice of the Divine order of things. Instead of following God's commands with humility he kept on reasoning and became a pacifist.

At that time, it was in 1939, he was called up for military service. Eric was very unhappy. He protested that he didn't want to leave his home. He revolted against authority and regarded its actions as calamitous. In this way he questioned the Divine will itself without which nothing can happen on this earth.

Still protesting and complaining he joined an infantry unit and together with his detachment left our city.

First he was sent to Poland. Every day the distance increased between him and his native city until one day he reached the Russian frontier. But his thoughts never left Hamburg and he was sad to be posted so far from home.

During the years that followed Eric Kraus had to go farther

and farther away from Hamburg. Not being very strong or tough he peevishly complained about the discomfort of the journey and, above all, grumbled against the war, as if war was not among the dispensations of Providence. With these blasphemies on his lips he continued his easterly advance.

When he reached the Caucasus his dissatisfaction with life was at its zenith. "*Verflucht!*" he shouted. "What good is all this? I'd give everything to be in Hamburg now. I can't understand why this damned war has dragged me out here."

Such were the words of Eric Kraus, not unlike those of all the unbelievers who are never satisfied with the lot assigned to them by Providence. But at that very moment it became clear why the Lord in His infinite mercy had made Eric suffer those trials.

A notification arrived for him from Hamburg. It announced the death of his wife and four children during an air raid on the city.

When Eric read this he fell on his knees and, raising his arms to heaven, exclaimed: "Thank you, O Lord. Now I know why you created the Wehrmacht and caused this war, why you've taken me so far from Hamburg in spite of my stupid protests. It was all because you wanted to save me. You wanted to make sure that I don't die in an air raid with my soul full of sin. And, unworthy as I am, I have grumbled and cursed. Forgive me, O Lord."

Eric Kraus has returned to Hamburg. But what a changed man he is. No longer does he complain about unforeseen orders of the authorities and he'll always vote for the Christian Democratic Party. He's no longer a pacifist because he remembers his miraculous escape. He's married again and his second wife has just given birth to their fourth child. Every morning at breakfast Eric, looking at the ceiling, says to his family: "Remember that whenever the moment of need comes and Herr Chancellor Adenauer orders general mobilisation, your father will be the first to go into battle."

And you, my brothers and sisters? What will you do?

II

MONOLOGUE

Joan, two more doubles, please. Not good for us? I know. Here you are.

The summer is over. Haven't heard a cuckoo for months. Do me a favour, please: cuckoo a few times. You don't? Neither do I.

I see that they are putting Mickiewicz on his feet again.[1] So what? I don't know. I've nothing against him. A man like any other. Cigarette? You don't smoke? Neither do I.

You know, winter has its bright side. Troika, sleigh, snow. . . . You just sit and speed past Russian villages. . . . And yet . . . Did you say anything? No? I'm not saying anything either.

You just can't overestimate the importance of nature. You buy a pelargonium and look at it. Your manager will cut your bonus or a tram will cut off your leg. And the pelargonium is still there. Your health! You aren't healthy? Neither am I.

When I was small I didn't like symphony orchestras. They seemed ridiculous. Do you remember "Si, si, si"? "Vagabond's Serenade"? We were going to have a war with Lithuania then, or something. The Colonels. It all passed happily. "Hey, friend, more life!" How I loved that song.

Joan, give us two more, please. Yes, doubles.

[1]Mickiewicz, Polish national poet, had many statues erected to his memory; some of them were damaged during the last war.

49

Isn't our history full of detail. Take the battle of Grunwald. One knew what one could afford. Personally I prefer red currants. Less trouble. But one mustn't eat too many. Not good for the tum.

Health is the most important thing. I'm absent-minded. Went into the lavatory and undid my collar. One's got to know how to live.

Take the depth of the ocean. Jelly-fish, eels, plaice all floating around. They want to drink something. But there's absolutely nothing to drink. Aren't we in a much happier situation? You don't drink? Neither do I.

Have a piece of cheese. It's lovely cheese, as beautiful as Capri or the Louvre. You don't like the Louvre? Neither do I. I feel an instinctive antipathy to it. That's why I'm keeping away from Paris.

You know, we may never meet again. I'm going to move to Wieliczka. They have Europe's most interesting salt mine there. One has to hang on to something. In the evening I'll look at the glare of light above Cracow. They are watchful, I'll say to myself.

I can't ride. But I ride on trams admirably. Even so I had an accident. No, nothing. Someone asked me: "What is it that you really want?" I couldn't tell him.

Joan, two more please.

"Fill all thy bones . . ." I've got toothache.

Art and life. One could say a great deal. Take a dachshund. "A dachshund sitting by a tree gazes at people with wonder. Not one of them knows where to search for the blissful and happy skies." Remember that passage? That's how it was.

Two more doubles, Joan.

I knew a producer once. Talented. Would you believe it, I've got rheumatism. It's from the water. The elements can be vicious when they want to.

I love planting forests. Every "Day of the Forest" is my day. A forest is health and milk.

Joan, same again, please.

My dear fellow, I've never suffered. Of course, sometimes you come across a hyena. You don't shake hands with him. Altogether we can rejoice, if there's a reason for it. You're losing your hair. So am I.

Do you know that depressing little poem about falling hair, a dying horse, a deserted farmhouse? By Jesienin, I think. It's got something, as someone has said pointing at his father's coffin.

Joan . . .

12

THE GIRAFFE

Little Joe (who looked rather funny because the hair on his head grew forward) had two uncles. They were very unlike each other.

The first uncle, the older one, lived in a narrow alley adjoining a nunnery. He occupied a large ground-floor room. ("I prefer the ground floor, my dear sir," he would say, "to all your new-fangled ideas, upper storeys and such-like.") His room was full of old books, the thick volumes occupying shelves half-eaten by woodworm before the grubs died of boredom.

On one occasion, when Joe was visiting his uncle, he knocked one of the volumes off a shelf, the heavy book fell on his head, and the uncle's daily help had to go to the chemist to buy a bandage. The title of this book was "Spirit against Matter".

Joe's uncle never left his room. He spent all his time sitting at a high desk and writing. What he wrote must have been interesting since he had been working on this very subject for forty years. Anyhow, the gist of this work was as follows: "A Short Description of the World *a priori*, or what would the world look like if the earth were not a sphere, and *vice versa*."

Once Joe asked his uncle: "Tell me, Uncle, what's a giraffe like?"

The uncle had no idea of the appearance of this animal.

Since the age of twenty he had been concerned exclusively with his great work and this did not allow him to leave the four walls of his room. Also his reading, apart from the abovementioned "Spirit against Matter", was confined to treatises on the subjects of the absolute idea, the absolute will, the subjective idealism of the world, atranscendentalism, preconception of impressions and solipsism.

You may of course ask: And what did he do until he was twenty?

Well, until he reached that age his sole preoccupation had been with acne on his face, which persisted in spite of the infinite hours he spent in front of his mirror. As to visiting the zoological gardens, he had never done so for fear of witnessing the immodest behaviour of the animals.

So his nephew's question took him by surprise, but he did not show it. After all, he was not an agnostic, but a pure metaphysicist. During his life-long studies he had acquired the certainty that the sum total of knowledge about the universe had from the beginning been revealed to man *a priori*. In those circumstances the knowledge of the appearance of a giraffe was a mere detail.

"Come tomorrow and I'll tell you."

After Joe had gone his uncle drew the curtains, lit a candle and placed a human skull on his desk. Half of the night he lay prostrate on the floor, the other half he devoted to study.

The following day Joe came back for his answer.

"You wanted to know what a giraffe is like," the uncle began. "Well, a giraffe is an animal with three legs, horns on its head, and a horse-like tail. It feeds exclusively on fungi with cream. Now, go away."

"And what does it eat in the winter, when there are no fungi?"

"In the winter it eats pickled mushrooms."

Joe thanked his uncle and went away. He had always been slightly afraid of this uncle and looked upon him with great respect. However, he was not quite satisfied with the information he had been given. Somehow the problem of the giraffe did not appear to have been settled satisfactorily. Mainly because of the fungi.

He decided to ask his second uncle.

As so often happens in families, there was no resemblance whatsoever between the two uncles. They even pretended not to know each other. The second uncle led a very active life, he was the editor of a newspaper. Because of this all-absorbing job he could never be found at home and little Joe telephoned him at the editorial office.

"Hullo, Uncle, this is Joe."

"What can I do for you, comrade?"

"Uncle, I just wanted to ask you to tell me what a giraffe is like."

"Look it up in the *Notes for Lecturers*."

"I have. There isn't a word about it."

"Well, then, what about *Feuerbach*?"

"We took him at school. It isn't there."

"Then look in *Anti-Duehring*."

"I have. No luck."

"It must be there."

"It isn't."

"Impossible. It must be in *Anti-Duehring*. You are imagining."

The uncle hung up.

When he was still a small boy, the same age as Joe, he had seen a picture of a giraffe. It was one in the series "Animals" which was distributed free as an advertisement for a firm of chicory merchants. The uncle thus had some sort of a notion of what a giraffe looked like but, as his knowledge dated back to the pre-war capitalist times, he was unwilling to admit it. He gave instructions not to be disturbed and he began to study his Marxist library. Soon he discovered that little Joe had been right. There was no mention of a giraffe in *Ludwig Feuerbach and the Twilight of Classic German Philosophy* or in *Anti-Duehring* or even in *Das Kapital*. The very word "giraffe" did not appear in any of those works.

When further research also proved fruitless the editor found himself in a quandary.

Should he admit his knowledge derived from the chicory advertisements? No. He did not want to. Admission would place him on a level lower than that of tens of thousands of people who before the war could not even afford chicory.

Should he then declare that he did not know what a giraffe looked like? Again, no. How could he? What about his reputation? Had he not adopted wholeheartedly the thesis of the perceptivity of the objective world and consequently had he not given the impression that he knew everything? Even if he did not know something he could not admit it.

Finally, there was the possibility of looking up the giraffe in a manual of zoology. This he ruled out without hesitation. To do so he regarded as narrow specialisation which inevitably led into the quagmire of objectivist science.

When little Joe telephoned again to enquire about the giraffe he was given the brusque answer: "There's no such thing as a giraffe."

"What? What do you mean, there is no such thing?"

"It doesn't exist. If you want, I can tell you what a dog or a rabbit looks like."

"But the giraffe . . . Why do you say it doesn't exist?"

"Because it doesn't. Neither Marx nor Engels, nor any of the great thinkers who have continued their work, say anything about giraffes. That means that the giraffe doesn't exist."

"But . . ."

"There can be no 'but'. I tell you . . ."

Joe replaced the receiver and sighed deeply. Then he consulted the young man who acted as the leader of his Boy Scout patrol.

The patrol leader was a normal young man. "Have you no bigger worries?" he said. "All right, wait till Sunday. We'll go to the Zoo and check it on the spot."

They went. They saw the giraffe. They discussed it. Joe thanked the patrol leader and, deep in thought, started for home. On his way he sold his school satchel and called at a florist's and at a stationer's.

Next day at noon a messenger entered the editor's office and delivered a bunch of roses accompanied by the following short letter:

"My dear brother,

"Why do you never come to see me? We could talk about our youth, the family, little Joe and giraffes. . . .

"God bless you.

"Your devoted brother."

The first uncle, who, after little Joe's visit, had resumed work on his *opus magnum*, found a dead mouse in his inkwell.

Little boys seldom have enough money for two bunches of roses.

56

13

THE PARSON AND THE BAND

Saturday. Late afternoon.

Outside the village church the band of the fire brigade is assembling. Hard-working bees flit among the blossom of lime trees. Now and again one of the bees strays into the horn of an instrument, bumps into the shiny metal for a while, and flies away with an angry buzz.

The band is here to give a concert.

Sound carries well in the still air and the horns are plainly audible throughout the small village. Outside their houses the peasants are sitting on their doorsteps, the more prosperous on benches. They are listening.

The band leader gives the sign.

The instruments respond.

The sound reaches the vicarage. In the vicarage lives a very old parson. He keeps away from politics. He collects plants instead.

Secular music reaches the parson's ears.

He picks up the stick without which he can hardly move. Slowly he makes his way from the vicarage to the church. He opens the gate of the churchyard. The ancient, rusty hinges creak. He stops. He puts his hand to his ear.

They are playing.

"Secular tunes in front of the House of God! Those good-for-nothing . . ."

The band plays on.

"I'll show them," mutters the good old parson. He is already by the second gate, the one that leads from the churchyard to the little square in front of the church. He sees the band: six helmeted firemen with brass instruments. The band leader sporting a feather on his helmet. Of course, youngsters want to show off.

"Rascals! Still, there were days when I was young." He remembers how in the seminary he used to play basket ball in the yard.

Still, they need scolding. After all, secular music right by the church.

The smell of lime blossom is strong. During the short pauses in the music, when the firemen draw breath into their lungs, one can hear the buzzing of the bees.

A great wave of understanding for men and their weaknesses fills the parson's heart. He has lived so long, seen so much. . . . Should we not be tolerant towards the shortcomings of our fellow men? Does the suffering in which men are born and die not compensate for such small frolics?

"Still, they shouldn't be doing it. How can they . . . ?" He is still a little angry.

The gate creaks. The firemen look round. They stop playing. The parson moves nearer. Silver-haired. Leaning on his stick. They bow reverently. He stops and, wagging his finger at them, says: "Now, now. . . ."

But there is laughter in his blue eyes as he turns towards the vicarage garden.

The firemen play on.

14

IT'S A PITY

"The weather is wonderful. The sun has excelled itself today and the procession passing our microphones is flooded by the bright warm light that comes down from the incredibly blue sky. On the branches of trees I can see birds, thousands of them. It's difficult to believe that we have so many birds. We spend our time grumbling and it takes a festive day like this, after years of mistakes and deviations, to make us realise how we abound in birds. Those birds are singing, they are singing so stupendously that it seems that they are not birds, but . . . horses.

"At this moment a group of sportsmen is passing the saluting base. Their muscles tensed, smooth and bulging. Torsos forward, loins thrown backwards! We are producing aluminium and we shall produce more. This is our youth. The youth that will not let us down. They are waving to the saluting base, they are shouting something, but I can't hear what. The singing of the birds drowns everything.

"The next group is approaching. The sportsmen are followed by old-age pensioners and children from orphanages. Their ranks mixed, symbolising their brotherhood, they are marching under the slogan 'Old age and youth—youth and old age'. Now they are marching past but until recently they'd been forgotten, unjustly forgotten. It's a pity you can't see them. Little blond heads side by side with striped or simple grey gowns, pyjamas or jackets! Wrinkles glisten in the sun. Some of the children haven't yet learnt to walk properly, so the organisers had to string them together in fives and tie them to the more vigorous pensioners. On the other hand those of the old folk who can't see well are guided by the chatter of the kids. Those kids are our wonderful new breed of foundlings. I can now hear the order 'Eyes right!' All those who had been paralysed on the right side, those with nervous twitches in their right arm, have been waiting for years for this very moment when they can show off. They are now passing the saluting base. One of the pensioners started to clap but one of his arms came off. A soldier picked it up and returned it to its owner. When the old man thanked him the soldier stood to attention and saluted.

"They've passed. But this isn't the end of the procession. By no means. We can already hear the noise of stamping and shuffling. Yes, here they come. Our glorious, incomparable rehabilitated invalids! A group of men with dark glasses and white sticks would have taken the wrong turning were it not for a spirited detachment of legless who are swinging their crutches with gusto. And so the whole detachment in harmony advances on the saluting base. Wooden legs reflect the sun. We can see moving scenes; two men who had lost an arm each get together so that they can clap; a mute tries to cheer, but he can't.

"Next, speeding in front of us, is a squadron of invalid carriages. How neatly they are manœuvred! The sun is reflected from the nickel-plated spokes of their wheels. So we are producing nickel, and shall produce still more. It's a pity that you can't see this spectacle.

"They've passed. The street is empty. But don't think that the parade is over. Not by any means.

"Now they are coming, those who would have been visible

had they not died. Yes, here they are. The sun is shining. They are all marching past now, all the victims of mistakes. Salutes from the stand. Birds are singing. And they march past as if they were alive. That's what I call bearing and . . . understanding. Gaily they carry their coffins, presenting them at the saluting base, so that my eyes hurt. Yes, there's no doubt about it; they are marching past. We are a great exporter of oak and we shall become an even greater one. They are marching, proud that the day has come at last. Birds are singing.

"It's a pity you can't see any of it."

15

I'M SUBTLE

The first time I saw her she was in the company of a Colonel, who came near to her and twirled his moustache with one hand while inserting the other hand deep into her blouse. Being a trusting sort of fellow and of serene disposition I was not surprised by the Colonel's action. I assumed that he had lost something and it was only natural for him to try to retrieve it. The idea that his behaviour could have an erotic significance never even crossed my mind until I heard him say to her: "Well, my pet?"

Ah, I thought, so she is not as unapproachable as I had imagined. This discovery was confirmed when the following day I saw her riding a horse in the company of three lieutenants. It was at that moment that within me sprouted the audacious desire to show that I was a man. During a whole week I was working myself up while waiting for a suitable opportunity to demonstrate my bravado. That moment came soon. Overcoming all my inhibitions I bowed to her on the promenade and, though terrified by my own audacity, I said with a pleasant smile: "Good morning."

This determined approach made her nod to me but, arching her eyebrows, she went on.

I was burning with shame. How could I have behaved with such brutality. Idiot. It served me right. I wanted to run after her to ask her forgiveness and explain that I did not mean to be rude, even though it must have seemed so to her in view of my vulgarity. It occurred to me, however, that to speak to her then and there would have been even more callous.

Just in case, I kept out of her sight for three whole days. That was why I assumed that what I had heard about troop movements was connected with manœuvres or similar exercises. I went out only in the evenings and walked along empty streets immersed in my dreams and resolutions. It was purely by chance that I saw her in the park as she was pushing her way through some shrubs. Fortunately, she was not alone. Otherwise I would have had to make up my mind to go up to her and seduce her. The presence of a squadron of cavalry made the decision superfluous.

The few days of separation had one adverse result: I was no longer sure when and where I could find her, apart from the shrubbery. I did not know which reception, hunt or ceremony of laying a foundation stone she would be attending, and it was that kind of event which seemed to me most suitable for developing the activities of a seducer.

Fate came to my rescue. While I was engaged in a conversation with a civilian I knew, he suddenly mentioned her name. Pretending cold detachment, I gently hinted at some interest in her person. My friend went to the window and whistled three times. "I keep her in the courtyard so that she doesn't disturb me," he explained.

When she came up to the flat my friend performed the introduction. I kissed her hand unmindful of the piercing look she gave me. My conversation was sparkling. I was showering her with epigrams. Encouraged by my own eloquence and the gathering dusk I decided to go further than I had ever done before. Inch by inch my hand moved nearer to her. Imagine my joy when her hand did not withdraw at the touch of mine.

Drunk by this, my first victory, I talked even more brilliantly while devoting myself to delicate caressing of her hand. My triumph would have been greater still had not that hand, which I had found so near to her waist as to make it indubitably hers, turned out to belong to my friend.

Later on I did not regret it as much as I had at first; six months after that encounter I found myself sitting next to her at a meeting, and when I took her hand into mine she withdrew it gently but firmly, adding, in a friendly yet stern manner, that she had not expected such behaviour from me. I was very much ashamed.

The next day I brought her some flowers. In the dark hall I tripped on a drum of the kind you see strapped to regimental drummers. I fell and bruised myself. She explained later that in any case she could not have seen me then as she was in bed with a horrible cold.

It must have been during the second spring of our acquaintance that she announced one day in passing that she would call on me at dusk to borrow some matches. I had seen her perhaps a score of times at various hunts, receptions and ceremonies of laying of foundation stones. This time I decided I must behave with ruthless brutality.

When she came she appealed to my sense of honour. Later she voiced her disappointment at discovering that I was just like all men; she had held me in high esteem and hated to be proved wrong. She asked about the matches. As I had clean forgotten about them I had to go out to buy a box so that I could lend it to her. She nodded to me. Out of emotion I saluted. She left.

I should not grumble. I am told that she speaks well of me. She says that I am very subtle.

16

THE MONUMENT

We have in our town a monument to the Unknown Fighter of 1905. He died at the hand of the tyrant during the revolution, and his fellow citizens made a little mound to commemorate him. Fifty years later a stone plinth was placed on the mound with a carved inscription "Eternal Glory". Above the plinth rose a statue of a young man breaking his chains. The unveiling of the statue in 1955 was performed with great ceremony. Lots of speeches. Masses of wreaths and flowers.

Some time later eight pupils from a local school decided to pay their homage to the unknown hero. Their eloquent history master had moved them so deeply with his description of the revolution that, after school, they pooled their money and bought a wreath. Forming a small cortège they walked towards the monument.

When they turned the corner of the street they met a short man in a navy blue overcoat. He looked at them and started following them at a distance.

They passed the old town square. People paid no attention to them. Processions are not unusual.

Few people live in that part of the town. There is St. John's Church but the old houses surrounding it have been converted into offices and museums.

When they reached the monument the man in the overcoat approached them quickly.

"Good evening," he called. "Paying your homage? Very nice. Very nice indeed. It is the anniversary? One is so snowed under by work that one cannot remember . . ."

"No, it isn't the anniversary. We just felt like it," answered one of the boys.

"What do you mean, 'just felt like it'?" The man's voice rose in surprise. "What do you mean by this?"

"We simply wish to honour the memory of a revolutionary who gave his life in the fight for the freedom of the people."

"Ah, so you are from the district committee of the Party."

"No, we are from the school."

"You mean, there's no one with you from the committee?"

"No."

He thought for a while. "Perhaps the school ordered you?"

"No, we decided by ourselves."

He went away. The boys were placing the wreath on the plinth when one of them called out: "He's coming back."

Indeed, the man in the overcoat had appeared again. This time he stopped a few paces away and asked: "Is it by any chance the month devoted to the deepening of respect for unknown revolutionaries?"

"No," they shouted back in unison, "we've decided by ourselves."

He walked away. The boys deposited the wreath and were about to go when the stranger returned. He had a policeman with him.

"Your identity cards, please," demanded the policeman.

They produced their school cards. He examined them and saluted.

"They are in order. Everything seems to be in order."

"Not at all," protested the man in the overcoat and, turning to the boys, he asked: "Who told you to lay that wreath?"

"No one."

66

He beamed. "So you admit it?" he cried. "So you admit that this demonstration in honour of the Unknown Revolutionary has been organised neither by your school, nor by the Praesidium of the Association of Polish Youth, nor by any committee of the Party?"

"Of course it hasn't."

". . . That this ceremony has not been initiated either by the League of Women or by the Society of Friends of 1905?"

"No."

". . . That it's neither the anniversary nor the special month, nor anything like that?"

"No."

". . . That you've had no directive at all? That you've done this all by yourselves?"

"Yes, we have."

He mopped his brow with his handkerchief.

"Officer," he said, "you know who I am. Remove this wreath. And you: go home!"

The boys left in silence. The policeman went off carrying the wreath. The activist in the navy overcoat was left alone by the monument. He was eyeing the statue with suspicion.

It started to rain. Small drops fell on his navy coat and on the stone jacket of the revolutionary. The clouds brought twilight in their wake. Silver drops were flowing down the face of the statue, hesitating on the ear lobes like ear-rings, glistening in the granite eye sockets.

And so they stood, facing each other.

17

THE BACKGROUND TO AN ERA

My new lodgings were in a street which for some fifty years had been one of the city's main arteries. The high ceiling of my ground-floor room seemed to be supported by a pair of exceedingly tall and narrow windows and a similarly elongated door with an ornate brass handle. Persistent twilight filled this room, defying the sunshine outside; only at noon would it recede momentarily into the corners and under the canopy of the ceiling, returning soon to occupy the whole room triumphantly. All I could see through my windows was a row of similar windows on the opposite side of the street, blind ones because of the gloom that filled the rooms behind them.

Just outside my window-sill the headgear of passers-by was floating about; it seemed as if the city had been flooded and the waters were carrying an endless stream of men's and women's hats, mementoes of their drowned owners. The constant rustle of footsteps that reached me through the closed windows kept on reminding me of a river.

One day, among the usual multitude of floating hats, I saw one quite unlike all the others: a black bowler. It passed my window and disappeared. The river flowed on. A minute or so later, when I answered the doorbell, I saw the bowler again; it was on the head of an elderly man who was wiping his feet carefully though the weather had been dry for a week and there was no mat outside my door. Raising his hat the stranger enquired if he might come in. Once inside he looked around, took out of his pocket a folded newspaper and announced: "I've brought the solution."

"What solution?"

He passed me the newspaper. It was the colour of old ivory dominoes. The type was of a style that had gone out of use a long time ago; the letters had long anaemic legs and their feet and heads were marked by thin horizontal lines. My eye caught the beginning of a despatch: "6th June, 1906. The current week in Baden Baden. . . ."

"The puzzle," he pointed, seeing my lack of comprehension.

On another page there was the puzzle and next to it the solution written out in a careful hand in a mauve copying pencil which had been licked in the process.

"I see."

"I've got the complete solution."

"Yes."

"I've brought it here as it says in the instructions. I could have posted it, but I thought I'd rather bring it myself. But is this the editorial office?" he asked, looking doubtfully at the furniture.

"No. It no longer is. It's now a private apartment."

"Pity. I've solved it all. And where is the editorial office now?"

I shrugged my shoulders.

"When I moved in it was already a private apartment."

"And before that?"

"I don't know."

"Great pity! I've solved it all by myself."

"Perhaps there was an editorial office here once," I said, "but it must have been a long, long time ago."

He nodded.

"Yes, fifty years ago."

The stupid man was beginning to irritate me.

"What do you want with your puzzle? Don't you know that a lot has happened since then?"

"I can't help it that I'm not an intellectual," he said in an offended voice, "but I've solved it all by myself."

We were both silent for a moment. It was only then that I noticed the name of his newspaper and became really indignant.

"Do you realise that your newspaper was a perfidious organ of a monarchy that followed a policy of dividing national minorities?"

"It happened on a Sunday," he said. "My uncle came to see us. He had this paper in his pocket. It was a hot day and we were sitting in the garden. Father and uncle decided to play cards. I wanted to join them, but Father wouldn't let me. He said I was too young and I would have enough time for playing cards when I was grown up. Then they took off their jackets; they left their waistcoats on. My uncle's jacket was hanging on a branch of a cherry tree, and when they started playing I took the paper out of his pocket. That's how I started on the puzzle."

"And you've only just finished," I added with irony.

"Yes. It was a very difficult puzzle. Do you know the word 'adequate'? And there were even worse ones."

"But what about the First World War?" I said.

"I was in a reserved occupation."

"You're funny! All those changes, upheavals, the republic, the referendum . . ."

"Do you think it was easy? Back in 1910 we didn't really know what a Zeppelin was. I couldn't figure it out. Only after I got 'zip' and 'pelt' and 'in', and that took some working out—only then did I begin to see daylight."

"You are impossible. The 1929 depression, and you still at your puzzle. . . ."

"Perhaps I'm not very clever. Maybe you think I had too much time. But I had to work, my dear sir, I had to earn my living. Only in the evenings could I get down to the puzzle."

"And what about the Spanish Civil War? What about Hitler? What were you doing then?"

"Haven't I told you? I've had to solve it all by myself. Lots of foreign words. It wasn't easy. Still, I've got a head on my shoulders."

"You are a wizard." I was mocking him. "Probably you spent the Second World War working on your puzzle. You are an Einstein, but you didn't invent the atom bomb. You didn't know how."

"The bomb is a different matter. That wasn't my responsibility. But do you think it's easy for an old man? One's forgotten all one's learned at school. And there are so many worries. But I never gave in."

I laughed loudly and derisively. He was offended. He rose and said: "You shouldn't laugh. I haven't invented the bomb, but there's nothing one can do about it. In nineteen-fourteen I was in a reserved occupation, but even before the war broke out I'd been hit in the head by a ricochet bullet. It was in Montenegro that it happened. You're laughing, but one should respect human thought. Here's the puzzle. Human thought isn't dead."

18

IN THE DRAWER

This morning, while searching for my glasses, I pulled out the centre drawer of my desk and noticed the little people who lived there. Between the case for my spectacles and an envelope of photographs stood a pleasant-looking young couple of tiny human figures. He, about the size of my thumb, had light-coloured eyes and was smiling. She, as big as my little finger, looked dainty yet agile; her golden hair tied at the back was just touching her shoulders. They had been looking at each other when I opened the drawer and they both turned to me with one movement. To them I must have been as large as God, powerful and heavy. I smiled at them. The smile was equivalent to a change in the weather. However, they showed no fear. Holding hands they advanced a few steps towards the edge of the drawer which was touching the sweater I was wearing. The newspaper with which the drawer was lined rustled under their feet. Carefully I bent my head, conscious that my movements might be like earthquakes to them. I could not see the expression in their eyes; they were the size of pinheads. They explained quite openly that they were in difficulties; her mother would not agree to their marriage. It sounded like an appeal for help.

Having just had my breakfast I was in a very good mood. In my drawer there was a whole world. Emotions. Problems. It was pure chance that I saw those two first. I discovered that they had many many relatives who also inhabited my drawer, living in their little houses. There was a whole street of those houses, perhaps even a whole town. I was surprised to find my drawer full of longings, love and hatred. . . . With a strange, but not unpleasant, sensation I realized that my hands and my voice had suddenly become involved in the lives of those miniature people. Unexpectedly I had become a great power which, having accidentally touched on their affairs, could now influence them in a decisive manner. They were so small that they meant nothing to me but I could be everything to them.

I repeat that I was in a very good mood and I took an immediate interest in their problems. I promised to intercede with the girl's mother. It gave me pleasure and satisfaction to anticipate the scene; what a great authority I would be in the woman's eyes! Having had a closer look at the drawer I discovered in it a horizon, the existence of which I had never suspected. I felt friendly and magnanimous. The August day promised to be fine. I joked with them, I laughed, I even went to the glass to look at my own eyes, grey-green and indecently large compared with their minute grains. At last, having politely indicated that I had to leave, I went out.

In the coffee house I met a man who had funny ideas about me. The sky clouded over and it began to rain.

The rain had stopped by the time I was on my way home, but the uneven surface of the road was covered with puddles. A passing lorry sent a spray of muddy water sideways. I tried to jump out of the way but my evasive action was in vain: my precious, brand new, light trousers were spattered with mud.

Back home I opened the drawer in search of a brush. When the minute young man saw me he made a sign that he wanted

to speak to me. With a shy smile he explained that it
was the right time for my intervention, that if I wanted to help
them . . .

I swept them all away with one impatient movement of
my hand.

19

A FACT

"I want to confess to you, Father . . . I'm not sure I'll be able to . . . Could you, Father . . . ? I've a husband."

. . . ?

"I beg your pardon? Oh, no. Really. Of course, we are married. The organ was playing and I wore a long white veil. There was incense and lilies. And I said 'yes', and everybody was happy, and Mummy was crying and . . ."

. . . ?

"Just a moment. I'm coming to that. I was a poor young girl. I had big eyes and long pigtails. He came in a car. He was big and so strong. He walked with me to the top of a hill and, in his clear, resonant voice, he spoke about the future. He had so many plans. I fondled the shiny metal buttons on his uniform. I liked touching them with my cheek and seeing myself reflected in them like in a mirror."

. . . ?

"Yes, yes, Father. Of course I knew it was vanity. I'm sorry. Then we got married."

. . . ?

"No, not at all. He didn't change after the wedding. He's always been firm but also most considerate. Of course, we had our disagreements, but never serious. We were almost always together, he practically never left me."

. . . ?

"But, Father, how can you? Really . . . Yes, I've heard about it, but he isn't. Never. Nothing like that at all."

. . . ?

"Perhaps. I don't know. But I'm the one who's come to confession, not he. Here I am in need of help . . . I need your advice . . . I want con . . . soling . . . No, I'm not crying. Take my hand, Father."

. . . ?

"Yes. Of course I married him because I was in love with him. Where have I sinned? Ask anybody about him. They'll all tell you how respected he is, how gifted, how worthy."

. . . ?

"Pardon?"

. . . ?

"No, never. Really never. I haven't been unfaithful to him, not even in my thoughts. I've been a faithful wife. Do you believe me, Father?"

. . . ?

"No."

. . . ?

"No."

. . . ?

"Again 'no'."

. . . ?

"So what's all this about? Father, I've come here. . . . No, it's impossible to believe it. After seven years of living with him. . . . Last summer we went on holiday. I'd persuaded him to take a rest. He's got an important job, much work, enormous responsibility, the whole country. . . . One morning, at breakfast, we were sitting opposite each other. Behind him was an open window. Through it I could see the garden, trees. . . . The wallpaper in the room was printed in a pattern of little flowers, tens of thousands of little pink flowers. When he was lifting his cup I looked at him. There was no special reason or purpose behind my gaze. And then I saw . . ."

. . . ?

"Yes, what did I see? How can it be that for seven years I'd shared his table and his bed, and only now . . . Do advise me, Father, because if it's a sin. . . ."

. . . ?

"It was only then that I noticed that he was made of plasticine."

. . . ?

"Yes. All of him. He's all artificial. I bent over him. My eyes must have been very wide open because he put down his cup and asked calmly: 'What's the matter?' No, I'm not mistaken this time. He's always been made of plasticine. All of him! Why, oh why had I never noticed it before? And now what's going to happen?"

. . . ?

"An annulment of the marriage? But, Father, that's impossible—we have children!"

20

A CONFESSION ABOUT BOBBY

A new school term is beginning and I think the time has come to tell all I know about Bobby. He has been haunting me for quite a while. Last time he appeared I had to sit down in a wicker chair and deliver a monologue about Bobby. It was the first moonlit evening after a series of clear nights that were illuminated only by the stars. Today I even know what Bobby looks like. He is pale, his large head is set on a thin neck, his ears stick out, and under a brush of hair a thoughtful forehead is at work.

The first subject that captured my helpless imagination, imprisoned it and tied it for ever to little Bobby was the business of the snail. Now, we all think that we know what a snail is. Bobby, however, approached the subject in a highly individualistic manner. Let us look at his exercise book. Under the heading "God bless" we can read his essay: "The snail is a small creature which supports itself by pushing out its horns. In return for this it receives a certain quantity of cheese with which it makes Welsh Rarebit."

At school Bobby asked: "And when a snail goes for a walk and wants to kick somebody, which foot does it use?"

The teacher replied: "Bobby, you ought to know that a snail only has one foot. Why didn't you pay attention when we learnt about it? Oh yes, I remember: you were sitting under the table."

Bobby was not put off. I must admit frankly: Bobby lies. When he returned home and was asked what was new at school, he said: "The teacher told us that a snail kicks with its left foot, but I pointed out that this couldn't be true since the snail had only a right foot. But the teacher wasn't paying attention. He was sitting under the table."

Bobby's mind was preoccupied with snails. A few days later he asked his uncle: "If a snail is about to be called up and wants to have two legs so that it passes the medical, can it borrow another leg from a friend?"

"No, Bobby, his friend also has one leg only. It would be left without anything. . . ."

"But couldn't his friend borrow a leg from a third snail?"

"No, because the third snail would be left without anything."

"Couldn't he borrow from the fourth?"

"It's late, Bobby. Go to bed."

"And the fourth from the fifth?"

"Run along, Bobby. Go and play in the yard."

"And the fifth from the sixth?"

"Bobby!"

"Uncle . . ."

"Yes?"

"If I were a snail I'd have three legs so that I could lend them to friends."

"Very good. It shows you have a kind heart."

Indeed. One day, when ginger Tommy was torturing some cats, Bobby said: "You just wait. When God catches you He'll show you!"

And yet there is something in Bobby that arouses suspicion. Once he did not take off his cap on entering his form. The teacher admonished him: "Why don't you take your cap off?"

"Because Mummy says I mustn't take it off or I'll catch a cold."

When he got home he said: "Mummy. I've got a cold because the teacher ordered me to take off my cap."

The following day he was absent from school. When he appeared the day after the teacher asked: "Why did you miss school yesterday, Bobby?"

"Because Mummy says 'East, west, home's best'."

In due course their studies reached the point when the teacher explained how man learnt to protect himself from the cold by using wool and animal fibres and making warm clothes and headgear.

Bobby digested this information and declared: "My daddy always wears a hat because, he says that if ever he walks by a lake and falls into the water the hat will float on the surface and they'll know where to find him."

After further thought he added: "We already have a place for him in the family grave. Auntie says it's so much gayer to stick together."

Such is Bobby. Beware of him. He is nice, but . . .

Soon we shall have the full moon again.

21

A DRUMMER'S ADVENTURE

I loved my drum. I carried it suspended from a wide strap across my shoulders. It was a big drum. I used oak sticks to strike its matt, yellow membrane. With time the drumsticks had acquired a polish from my fingers, testifying to my zeal and diligence. I carried the drum along roads white with dust or black with mud; the world on either side was green, golden, brown or white according to the season. Wherever I went the landscape reverberated with a rat-a-tat-tat, for my hands did not belong to me but to the drum and when the drum was silent I felt ill. Thus one night I was drumming gaily when the General came up to me. He was incompletely dressed in his uniform jacket, which was unbuttoned, and his long underpants. He greeted me, hummed and hawed a little, praised the Government and the State, and at last said casually: "And you just go on drumming, do you?"

"Yes, sir," I shouted, striking the drum with redoubled force. "To the glory of our country."

"Quite right," he agreed, but somehow his voice sounded a little sad. "And how long will you go on?"

"As long as my strength lasts, sir," I shouted back gaily.

"Good boy," he said, scratching his head. "And will your strength last much longer?"

"To the very end, sir," I said proudly.

"Well, well. . . ." The General sounded surprised. For a

while he seemed to be deep in thought and then he went off on a tangent.

"It's late," he said.

"It's late for the enemy, never for us," I shouted back. "The future belongs to us!"

"Very good, very good..." said the General, but he sounded cross. "When I said it was late, I meant that the hour was late."

"The hour of battle has struck! Fire the guns, ring the bells!" I shouted with the enthusiasm becoming a true drummer.

"Oh, no, not the bells," he said quickly. "I mean, let the bells ring, but only from time to time."

"Quite right, comrade General," I agreed with passion. "We don't need bells if we have our drums. Let the roll of my drum silence the bells!" To underline my point I struck a loud roll.

"Never the other way round? What?" asked the General. He sounded uncertain of himself and he was covering his mouth with his hand.

"Never, sir," I shouted back. "You can rely on your drummer, sir. He'll never allow his drum to go silent." I was carried away by a burning wave of zeal.

"Our army can be proud of you," the General said without enthusiasm. A cold fog had come down on our camp and he was shivering. All I could see in the grey mist was the top of the General's tent. "Yes, proud," he went on. "We shall never stop, even if we have to march day and night, even if... Yes, each step..."

"Each step will be an endless victory roll," I interjected, drumming for all I was worth.

"Well, well," murmured the General. "Yes, just that..." and he went towards his tent. I was left alone. Solitude stimulated my desire for self-sacrifice and my sense of responsibility

as a drummer. You've gone, General, I thought, but your faithful drummer is alert. With your brow furrowed you're working on your strategic plans, placing little flags on the map to mark the road to our joint victory. Together, you and I shall conquer the future and on your and my own behalf I shall announce the victory with a roll of drums.

I was overcome with tenderness towards the General, and with such a will to give myself to the cause that, if it were possible, I would have drummed even louder. In the depth of the night, fired by my youthful enthusiasm, animated by our great ideal, I devoted myself to my honourable task. From time to time, in between drum-beats, I could hear from the direction of the General's tent the creaking of mattress springs as if somebody, unable to sleep, were tossing in bed. At last, about midnight, a white figure loomed in the mist by the tent. It was the General in his night-shirt. His voice was hoarse.

"I say, so you're going to continue drumming, are you?" he asked. I was really moved that he should have come to me in the middle of the night. A true father to his soldiers!

"Yes, sir. Neither cold nor sleep will defeat me. I'm ready to go on as long as my strength lasts, obedient to the call of my duty and of the cause we're fighting for. My honour dictates it. So help me God!"

In saying these words I was not motivated by a desire to appear as a stickler for my duty or by a wish to suck up to the General. This was no empty boast on my part, calculated to bring promotion or any other reward. It never even crossed my mind that such an interpretation could have been put upon my attitude. I have always been a sincere, straightforward and, damn it, let me say it, a good drummer.

The General gnashed his teeth. I thought he was cold. Then he said: "Good, very good," and went away.

A few minutes later I was arrested. The patrol assigned to

this task surrounded me silently. They took my drum away, they removed the drumsticks from my cold and tired fingers. Silence filled the valley. I could not talk to my comrades who surrounded me with their rifles pointing at me, that was not allowed by regulations. They led me out of the camp. On the way one of them whispered that I had been arrested on the General's orders. The charge was treason. Treason!

Dawn was breaking. A few pink clouds floated in the sky. They were greeted by healthy snoring which I heard as we passed the General's tent.

22

THE CO-OPERATIVE

The manager answered the telephone. "Hullo . . . Yes . . . Yes . . . Victory Street? Yes, indeed. He'll be along presently."

He replaced the receiver.

"As you can see," he said, "we can't complain about lack of customers. I must go now, and see my staff. Would you like to come with me?"

The offices of Co-operative One were situated in what used to be a private apartment. The premises had been hurriedly converted, the front room, which had a balcony, becoming the manager's office. We went into the corridor and entered a small room. Once this had been a bathroom, a very large one. The bath was still there and by it a large recess gaped with naked bricks; it used to house the gas geyser. In the yellow light of a weak bulb I could see benches arranged along the tiled walls. Sitting or lying on the benches were several men, faded individuals in soiled suits. Most of them were asleep, but a few were consuming a snack of beet soup and pickled gherkins.

"Who's next?" asked the manager from the door.

A middle-aged man rose from one of the benches. He had thinning hair and swollen eyelids.

"What's the address, boss?" His voice was hoarse.

"Number three, Victory Street. Call at the shop."

"Right." The man started buttoning his coat.

We returned to the manager's office. On the wall was a poster announcing a year of celebrations in memory of a national poet.

"The principles of our organisation are very simple," explained my host. "The low fees paid by our customers cover our running expenses, the telephone, the salaries of the manager, accountant and charwoman. The surplus goes to the School Building Fund."

"And the other employees?"

"That depends. As a matter of principle we rely on amateurs. You saw them in the waiting-room. They work on a rota which ensures that someone is available at any time of day or night. They are engaged on the understanding that their remuneration will be entirely in kind. In other words we only act as a go-between. We do have, however, a certain proportion of professional and highly qualified collaborators."

"How did you come to form the Co-operative?"

"Ah, well. How many men need company at all times of day and night. We all know, from our own experience, what it's like when one wants a drink but there's no suitable companion. For instance, you're drinking with a friend, but he has to leave. You accompany him to the station, you come back, and what? Terrible solitude. Or you've a day off. It's still before noon. Your friends are at work, the pubs are deserted. You're condemned to loneliness. Or late at night worry won't let you sleep, you've bought a bottle of vodka and you're sitting alone in front of an empty table. Well, here you have only a few of the endless number of situations when solitude, so distasteful to drinking men, can become a real nuisance. It's in these situations that our Co-operative offers a simple and effective remedy. We banish the fear of being left alone, we render unnecessary the frantic search for friends who often can't or won't drink with us. Just ring us up, give your address. Without delay one of our men comes to you, devoted, ready for his task, friendly, sympathetic, prepared to talk about anything, willing to listen to your worries, and, what's most important, a man who'll never say 'no'. We recruit only really suitable men who also want a drink but can't pay for it. Our task is to produce the key to mutual understanding. Thanks to us, those who want to drink and have the liquor get together with those who have none but feel the same need. Were it not for our Co-operative those two sets of men would pass each other in the streets, thirsty and sad, with as much chance of coming to an understanding as two galaxies in the sky."

"I call that humanism."

"Yes, but it's more than that. We also play a not unimportant economic rôle. The State operates the Alcohol Monopoly and we help to increase its turnover. Just think of all those bottles that would remain full were it not for us. It's a well-known fact that in company one drinks better, with greater pleasure and more."

At that moment the front door was slammed with a bang and in the hall a husky male voice started humming, "Don't go, don't go to the wood. . . ."

"Excuse me," said the manager. "One of our men has come back. I must hear his report."

A man was carried into the office. With an experienced movement the manager emptied a bucket of water over him.

"Returning from number twelve, Embankment of Heroes," reported the newcomer. "Export quality vodka. His wife had left him. He had a difficult childhood. Pneumonia in forty-eight. Ep! The world's lovely, he says, only people are bad."

"There you are," said the manager as his tired minion left the office, singing the "Blue Danube". "Another man saved from solitude."

"You did mention professional, highly qualified collaborators."

"Yes. Sometimes we've choosy customers. Some, for instance, see everything in a lyrical mood. I send them poets. If we get a call from a University professor, a specialist in the Maya culture, I can't send him just anybody. Then, there are men who like discussing religion over a glass of vodka. So I've in reserve a clergyman manqué, who had to leave the seminary. In other words, we keep in touch with all sorts of experts who undertake work for us."

The telephone rang. The manager quickly picked up the receiver.

"Co-operative One," he announced. "Can I help you?"

As he was listening, his face adopted a worried expression. He covered the microphone with his hand and turned to me: "It's a client in All Souls' Square. He wants someone with whom he could discuss the perspectives of socialist morality development. Where on earth can I get him one?"

"What's there to drink?" I asked.

"Just a moment." And into the telephone: "Can you, please, tell us what liquor is available for this occasion?"

He listened to the reply and, covering the microphone once more, informed me: "Cognac and cherry brandy."

"I'll go," I volunteered.

"Splendid!" exclaimed the manager. "I happen to have a vacancy."

He spoke into the telephone: "Order accepted."

23

PEER GYNT

By the stream stood a cabin guarded by a slender silver birch. In the cabin a young man lived with his wife. They loved each other. The wife said: "The roof needs mending; there's a hole in it and the rain comes through."

"It will be mended," he replied, following her with loving eyes.

The next day an important meeting was to take place in the nearby district town. The young man, who lived by the stream, had to drive his cart to the town because he had an important passenger, the headmaster of the local elementary school. His pretty wife was in tears when he said goodbye to her; she did not want him to go away.

In town, once he reached the assembly hall decorated with paper flowers, once the band struck up "We are building a new house", the young man quickly forgot his wife's tears.

"If there are any shortcomings you know of," said the chairman of the meeting, "you should speak out. Now, who wants to address the meeting?"

The young man, who was sitting by the door and listening with attention to the proceedings, was responsive to all appeals because of his simple and honest nature. "Me!" he shouted. "I want to speak."

They asked his name and social origin. "Peasant," he said. A murmur of approval went round the hall. People were craning their necks to see him walk to the rostrum. A journalist from the county town, who had been dozing comfortably, woke up and wrote in his notebook: "A peasant leader mounts the rostrum."

"Who is he?" enquired the secretary of the district committee of the headmaster.

"A driver. I've no idea what's possessed him."

"My dear fellow," the county Governor congratulated the District Officer, "he's a real peasant."

The young man rested his hands on the rails of the rostrum. To address such a big gathering was a great effort for him; he found no pleasure in the prospect but it did not even enter his head that he could have ignored the chairman's appeal. He said: "Well, I don't know much about this or that but I want to ask a question: why have we no roof tiles or nails in our village? We know that roof tiles and nails get here, to the district town, but it seems that our village is too far. But we, in our village, do need tiles and nails. That's all I wanted to say."

Stormy applause greeted his last words. The Governor, the District Officer, the Secretary of the Party, the headmaster, everybody was cheering. The journalist, leaning over his notebook like a rider over his speeding horse's neck, wrote: "That sturdy fighter . . ." The Governor, his face pink with pleasure, quickly went to the rostrum.

"Comrades!" he shouted. "Let's give our sincere thanks to our peasant comrade for his brief, peasant contribution to our meeting."

"Hear, hear!" from the audience interrupted this oration. The meeting was deeply moved.

"You are doing wonderful work here," said the Governor later to the District Officer, placing his arm on his subordinate's shoulder. Some people started singing the "Internationale".

The young speaker returned to his seat by the door. He did not understand the reason for the ovation. The question of roof tiles and nails seemed important to him and yet it was not even mentioned in any of the following speeches.

Little girls in national costume recited a poem and the meeting was over. The hall began to empty. Two strangers approached the young peasant who was still sitting in his modest corner.

"We want you to do us a favour," said the stouter of the two. "We heard your speech. Tomorrow in . . . (here they named the county town) we are organising an important meeting of the Food Co-operative and we'd like you to take part in the summing-up."

"You realise," added the second stranger with severity, "that this is a matter of political importance; the participation of the working peasants!"

"It will give you no trouble at all," insisted the first stranger, "and for us it will make all the difference. Another opinion. And the press reports will look so much better."

A friend took his cart and horse back to the village while the young peasant spent the night at the local hotel at the expense of the Food Co-operative. In the morning he travelled with the two strangers to the county town. He expected to be able to raise the question of roof tiles and nails with greater effect when he addressed the members of the Co-operative.

The meeting in the county town very much resembled that of the previous day. At a certain point the two leaders who had brought him there gave him a sign. He went to the rostrum and made his passionate appeal for roof tiles and nails for his village. Again he was given an ovation, but no practical measures followed.

After the meeting the stouter of the two Co-operative leaders thanked him for his performance and advised him to stay on in the town. "You may have noticed," he said, "posters advertising a meeting of artists. I'd go there. It's a bigger hall and the people will be more intelligent."

He really wanted to go home but there was no train till the evening. Dazed and bewildered by the city he thought of the artists' meeting as a safe refuge. He was becoming used to meetings, having attended two in quick succession. What is more, he no longer feared speaking in public and even found certain pleasure in anticipating the cheering that would reward his words.

At the artists' meeting he found that women were wearing trousers and men were clad in green or red shirts. This put him off, but he screwed up his courage and, when the moment came, he asked to be allowed to speak. When they enquired about his social origin, he shouted "Peasant". He was not disappointed. Amid general enthusiasm he told them about the non-existent roof tiles and nails. He was not sorry to have followed the advice of the Co-operative leader; the assembled artists did not lose interest in him when the meeting was over; some even began to sculpt him. One of them, however, a man of tremendous stature, led him away to a restaurant.

That artist, who had never attended any college, was making vast sums of money by running a team of art students to whom he passed for execution his numerous commissions for portraits. (It must be admitted that he also handed over to the students seventy per cent of his fees.)

When they reached the restaurant the artist suggested that the young peasant should stay on in town and attend a meeting to commemorate a national poet.

"But what about my wife and my leaky roof?" objected the peasant.

"It won't rain today," said the artist. "It's sure to be fine. Do it for me, be a good boy. . . ."

The whistle of a train sounded above the city.

The commemorative meeting took place in the theatre. In

the wings, among the scenery for Leoncavallo's *Pagliacci*, the painter gave him final instructions.

"Your entry is good, but you must stamp your feet a bit louder. When you shout that you're a peasant, you must do it with more zest; sound happy and proud. Now, about your text. This needs improving from the ideological point of view. Start with the words, 'We smallholders . . .' and then go into your business of tiles and nails. And when you finish shout, 'Three cheers for China!' "

Rain was coming down in buckets from the grey skies as the meeting ended. In the lobby the painter was waiting for him accompanied by delegates of the cosmetics industry. They were holding their meeting the following day.

The end of the week found him travelling in a third-class compartment to a meeting organised by the oil-prospecting industry. The din of the train reminded him of the clapping of audiences. In spite of himself he looked at his reflection in the window. The train was carrying him farther and farther away.

He bought a fitted suitcase. There was no difficulty about accommodation. As a participant in meetings, conferences and conventions he had his hotel and subsistence taken care of. He knew how to live economically.

No longer was he bound to the text of his original speech; he departed freely from it, adding many more improvements of his own to the corrections suggested by the painter. Thus he got into the habit of following his reference to the village being too far with the appeal: "Let's all join in the fight for our common catch-crops!" He would end his speeches either with the foolproof "Three cheers for China!" or simply with "China! China!"

He began to distinguish between various degrees of success and react accordingly. A welcome awaited him everywhere because, unfailingly, irrespective of the mood of the gathering, he would bring to it a healthy whiff of class, which was highly appreciated by the organisers. What he said also met the requirements of the authorities as far as criticism was concerned. Small wonder that he was accorded varied and rich literary treatment in the numerous press accounts and reports of his speeches. Thus time passed.

His new life was obliterating his memories of the old. He began to part his hair. Endless journeys, railway stations, conventions, conference halls, open-air meetings, formed the pattern of his daily routine. He became a member of a score of committees, he was invited to join praesidiums of meetings, he became a social governor of a kindergarten. Journalists and drivers of official limousines knew him well.

His habits also underwent a change. He learnt how to use the railway time-table and occasionally he would buy a bottle of eau-de-Cologne. But from time to time, when, lulled into sleep by the memory of the speeches at the last meeting he had attended, he was resting in his hotel bed, he would wake up suddenly to the sound of raindrops striking the window panes.

In due course he achieved a considerable degree of precision, perfection and drive in the work on which he was engaged. Self-confident, he no longer feared even national conferences. Meetings, festivals, praesidiums whirled round in his mind with such velocity that on one occasion he could not recall how he came to be sitting in a car, surrounded by elderly, bearded comrades in black suits. The car moved silently, one of a procession of similar vehicles. They crossed the city, passed the suburbs and in the gathering dusk drove across the countryside. After a long journey they stopped at a gate which swung open noiselessly, revealing a courtyard and a vast garden, almost a park, with trees and lawns brightly illuminated by floodlights. The night was clear. They mounted some steps, passed along corridors until they found themselves in a hall so large that its walls were invisible in the darkness. Only one small light was burning on the chairman's table, and even it was smothered by a metal shade. There was no ceiling. In the black sky stars were shining like frozen raindrops. The bearded comrades took their places in easy chairs.

One of them greeted the assembly and asked who wanted to speak first.

"I," shouted the young peasant. "I want to speak."

Nobody enquired about his social origin.

"We smallholders . . ." he began and paused for the inevitable cheers. There were none. "We smallholders!" he shouted louder. "We don't know much about this or that. But we do know that roof tiles and nails get to the district town, but they don't get to the village. And people . . ."

The deathly silence of the assembly made him stop. The chairman said: "This is a congress of astronomers. It appears that you are not one of us. Who are you?"

"I am a peasant."

"A peasant? Show me your hands."

He moved his hands into the lamplight. Everyone could see them clearly; they were white, the delicate skin showing no trace of heavy manual work.

Ushers removed him from the meeting. Celestial bodies watched the scene silently, their cold lights twinkling.

By the stream grows a silver birch. In its shade stands a cabin. Wind and rain have made a hole in the cabin's roof, spreading dampness and decay. A woman, prematurely aged by longing, sits on the doorstep watching the road, awaiting her husband's return.

When at last he does come back he is changed; his hair is parted, he carries a smart case. She runs to him but he does not embrace her. He only says with conceit:

"We smallholders . . ."

24

LETTER FROM AN OLD PEOPLE'S HOME

Our old people's home is humming today like a veritable beehive. When they brought me downstairs I noticed, hanging on the wall of our dining-room, a new issue of *Lightning*. And can you imagine who was the target of its attack? Our secretary himself, Comrade Glus. It nearly took our breath away, because Comrade Glus, though a youngster of seventy or so, has been ruling us for the past five years with an iron rod. It was he who, on the anniversary of the Revolution, launched the slogan that each of us should undertake to die prematurely, before our number came up. Still, he is not above quietly accepting a treat should someone secretly offer him a dish of gruel. People say that he is prepared to do anything for a plate of gruel.

In nineteen fifty-two during a solemn, commemorative meeting our colleague Pyz, who is stone deaf, shouted in good faith, "God save our Tsar Nicolai." Glus immediately drew certain conclusions from this incident. We do not know exactly what happened but two strangers came and placed a seal on colleague Pyz's set of dentures which Comrade Glus had left on a bedside table. Pyz's fate remains unknown to this day. The seal is still on the dentures.

People with a past have been particularly afraid of Glus. Old Pac-Pacynski, for instance, who had been wounded by

97

the partisans, had to put down in the questionnaire that it was Colonel Beck who had caused the injury because of Pac-Pacynski's opposition to the pre-war régime. Our colleague Kaczka, whom Glus denounced at a meeting for practising Swedish drill, broke down and dyed his beard bright red. Then take the case of our colleague, Miss Noga. As long as anyone can remember she has been wearing her hair in plaits. Suddenly Comrade Glus discovered that her plaits were a form of mockery of the Chinese, that she was in fact making fun of People's China. Miss Noga saved herself only by undertaking to knit a banner with a May Day slogan.

My own experience has been pretty chequered. As I knew how to play the balalaika, Comrade Glus made me the chairman of our Mitshurin circle. That in itself was not too bad because it let me off all the obstacle races, but on one occasion, when we had an inspection, I had to swallow two pounds of lead shot, just to prove that we had managed to grow special bilberries in dry, artificial surroundings.

We all remember the day when Mary Etual had the misfortune to drop her handbag and out of it fell her powder compact. Now, Mary Etual is about the same age as Comrade Glus and consequently deserves to be treated with a certain amount of forbearance. But Comrade Glus decided that this was an occasion for putting us all in our places. The result was that we all fell under suspicion of having pro-Gomulka leanings; and as for Mary Etual, when she got over the crisis, she took to writing poems in praise of smallholders. I should have one of her poems somewhere because Comrade Glus ordered us all to learn it by heart. Now, where can it be? Oh yes, here it is:

> Smallholder, listen to me,
> Your fate is as hard as can be,

You cannot sow, that is plain,
But you have to deliver the grain.

It is a lovely poem, isn't it?

I could tell you lots of stories about Comrade Glus. Once there was a terrible storm, but our colleague Tran pooh-poohed it, saying that he had experienced a much worse storm back in 1880. Comrade Glus immediately accused him of being a malcontent and of hankering after old times. I should tell you that Glus himself is suffering from a liver complaint and he invariably refers to it as "that cursed heritage of capitalism". On another occasion he made us all sign a petition to the authorities asking that our institution be called no longer just "Old People's Home", but be re-named "The Volga Home for Old People".

Now that you have some idea of what sort of a person Comrade Glus is you can appreciate why we have been afraid of him and what it meant to us this morning to find his methods under attack. We all crowded round the copy of the *Lightning* to see with our own eyes. Indeed, at the bottom of the page, in the left-hand corner, there was a paragraph which mentioned that Comrade Glus snores loudly during the night. Yes, that is what it said. . . . Times have changed.

25

GOLDEN THOUGHTS

Negro singers usually have hoarse voices; this hoarseness is due to the terrible housing conditions in which they are forced to live.

* * *

Obsession: a session on the river Ob.

* * *

The slogan of post-Communism: "Peoples of all the planets unite!"

* * *

Snow: powdered water.

* * *

You cannot hear the sea in every shell.

* * *

Man thinks this and that, but more often this.

* * *

Suicide: when a man puts a pistol, instead of the telephone, to his head.

* * *

A lover's disappointment: when a necrophil finds that his partner is only in a coma.

26

THE LAST HUSSAR

An air of secrecy and importance surrounded Bunny. Some of his acquaintances knew something but very few people knew all. Only Bunny's wife, his mother and his grandmother knew all. The rest, his relatives, even his children, were condemned to conjecture.

Every night, after the children had gone to bed, and Bunny in his slippers was sitting by the lamp with his newspaper, his wife would kneel by him, place her head on his knees and, gazing into his eyes, she would whisper, "For goodness' sake, Bunny, do be careful. . . ."

Bunny could not stand broth made with veal bones. Nor could he stand the régime.

Bunny is a hero.

Sometimes he returns home beaming but silent. His nearest and dearest know that if he wanted to, and if he could, there would be a great deal to tell them. In the evening his wife, timidly, with undisguised admiration, asks him: "Again?"

Bunny nods his head and stretches his arms. His whole bearing suggests masculine strength.

"Where?" asks his wife, surprised by her own audacity.

Bunny gets up and goes to the door. He opens it with a jerk to make sure nobody is listening behind it. He checks the curtains. In a low voice he answers: "The usual place."

"You," says his wife.

That one short word expresses everything.

As we have already mentioned, among his friends Bunny enjoys a somewhat unclear but exciting reputation: "Bunny must be careful. . . ." "Is Bunny in some danger . . . ?" "Bunny is showing them where they get off. . . ."

His mother is worried about him. Worried but proud. She always refers to him as "my son". His grandmother, a steadfast old lady who lives alone, is only proud. She never shows any fear or even worry. To her daughter, Bunny's mother, she says: "In our age one has got to take risks. Our cause needs fearless men. If Eustace were alive today he would be doing exactly as Bunny does."

Speaking to her great-grandchildren she says: "Be proud that you have a father like these"—here she shows them pictures of plumed knights galloping across a plain. "Your father could do the same. He hasn't broken down."

Meanwhile Bunny goes into a public convenience. Carefully he locks the door behind him. His gleaming eyes inspect the little cubicle. Is he alone? With a lightning movement he takes a pencil from his pocket and writes on the wall, "Down with Communism!"

Quickly he leaves the convenience and jumps into the first taxi or horse-cab that comes his way. He is driven away, but not in the direction of his apartment. He gets out and in a roundabout way goes home. In the evening his wife enquires shyly: "Again?"

Bunny has been acting in this way for a long time now, and though this dangerous life has affected his nerves and brought insomnia, he will not give up.

He is careful and always changes his handwriting. From time to time he also borrows his superior's fountain pen. "Should they trace back the pen, ha, ha, ha. . . ." He laughs ominously at the thought of his chief's discomfort, at the prospect of misleading his, Bunny's, persecutors. The tyrants.

Sometimes danger freezes the blood in Bunny's veins. It looks like the end. Once, for instance, while he was writing on the wall "Catholics will not give in!" there was a loud knocking on the door. Bunny's heart missed several beats. He was sure that THEY had come for him. Hastily he wiped off the slogan. The knocking continued. Bunny swallowed the pencil. He opened the door. Outside stood a stout man with a red face. He was clutching a brief-case. The public prosecutor? Without a word he pushed Bunny to the side, entered the convenience and locked the door. Bunny has not forgotten that experience. . . .

He viewed all lavatory attendants with the greatest suspicion. You never knew if one of them was not a disguised police spy.

One winter day he was marching towards his usual battlefield when an unexpected sight made him stop dead. The door of the convenience was shut. Across it, written in chalk, was a brutal notice, undoubtedly the work of the enemy. "CLOSED FOR REPAIRS."

Bunny felt like a hussar who, in the confusion of the battle, loses his sword.

But he decided to fight on. He went to the railway station. There he found a platoon of soldiers making in the direction of his goal. His suspicion was aroused. So not only have they used the treacherous subterfuge of "CLOSED FOR RE-PAIRS" but they have declared a state of emergency. In his mind he could see troops occupying all the public conveniences. But he was too clever for them. He could see through their clumsy designs. They would not get him.

Certain that all the objectives in the town must have been occupied, including Hotel Polonia and the communal canteen,

"Gastronome No. 1", he decided to strike elsewhere. The last word would belong to him.

He boarded a train, got off at the first stop and walked to the small, poor village he could see down in the valley. When he reached the first house he asked for the privy.

"What?" They were surprised. "We go into the bushes," they said.

It was already getting dark in the thicket. All the better, he thought. He went into the bushes and there with a stick he wrote in the snow: "General Franco will show you!"

He returned home. That night he stood for a long time in front of a mirror wondering if hussar's wings would suit him.

27

HORSES

A family matter took me to the town of N——. I had received a letter from there, full of spelling mistakes, obviously written by a hand unused to the pen. In it an unknown good soul informed me that the director of the State Stud had removed the remains of my grandfather, an insurgent of 1863, from their place of honour in the cemetery to make room for the body of his secretary whom everybody knew as his mistress. There was no signature on the letter, its author pointing out that he was already taking risks by informing me of this affair.

Having obtained two days' leave I went to N——. I had never been to the little town before. On arrival I sought out the house of the local grave-digger. He was not in and his wife informed me that he had just gone to the smithy to shoe a horse. I decided to wait for him on the bench by the cemetery wall. At last he appeared. He was a large, dour-looking man. He was leading a horse, or rather a pony, with a shining coat, its new shoes ringing now and again when they struck a stone. When he learnt the reason for my arrival the grave-digger became even more morose, threw me an evil look and declared that he knew nothing about it. After this brief speech he turned and disappeared behind the cemetery gate.

I decided to go to the town hall. In front of the building there was a pony tied to a pole. The Mayor received me and listened to my story but told me that he was much too busy to do anything about it. When I pressed him all the same, he took a different line.

"I don't know," he said, "if you are aware that the town council has adopted a resolution to replace your grandfather's remains by the body of a Korean partisan, which we are especially planning to bring over here. I assume that you don't question the political correctness of this decision?"

He looked at me searchingly.

I left the town hall in an agitated state of mind and went directly to the offices of the District Council. The chairman was an energetic young man with clear eyes. When I told him about my encounter with the Mayor he sounded angry.

"Yes," he said, "there is much room for improvement among the lower ranks of our authorities. Yes. Your grandfather? I've heard something about this matter. We shall try to clear it up, but . . ."

"But?"

"But it will take time . . ."

At that moment, from behind the door of his office, we could hear the loud and sprightly neighing of a pony.

The chairman's eyes performed a worried kind of dance. My heart felt the icy grip of foreboding. I turned and ran out.

The grave-digger and his pony. The pony outside the town hall. The neighing inside the District Council. I began to associate ponies with the opposition I met every time I tried to sort out the matter of my grandfather's remains. There must be some sort of a connection between breaches of the law and the breed of those small horses. Deeply immersed in the contemplation of this mystery, I walked towards the offices of the Front of National Unity. When I reached the building I noticed outside the door a carriage drawn by two lovely ponies. Slowly I retraced my steps.

Soon I discovered that the children of the local public prosecutor rode to school on ponies. Looking over the wall surrounding the garden of the President of Peasant Self-Help, I saw clear prints of small hooves. The Chairman of the Fighters' Association and the manager of the Delicatessen also owned ponies. What did it all prove? Defeated, I went to the railway station. Outside a policeman asked to see my papers. The policeman was riding a pony.

Some time later a paragraph in a newspaper caught my eye. "Following disciplinary proceedings, the director of the State Stud at N—— has been transferred to D——. It is reported that when inspectors arrived at N—— to investigate his activities he tried to bribe them with gifts of ponies."

A few weeks later I heard from D—— that my grandmother, an old suffragette, had been thrown out of the old people's home to make room for a former prostitute, who was the grandmother of the director of the State Stud.

I went to D——. When I knocked, the door of the old people's home was opened by a dwarf. He was holding the bridle of an enormous percheron.

28

POETRY

The mistress ordered them to take out their exercise books. In the front row little Helen, always a model pupil, complied at once. From her case she took a brand-new exercise book in brick-coloured covers and placed it on her desk. Helen was neither fat nor slim; she looked like an obedient child ought to look, like a girl who eats nourishing dinners without complaint. Her hair was plaited with precision; no question of unruly locks escaping the discipline. On her legs the stockings were properly stretched and straight. Her shoes were clean. It was clear at first glance that this girl would never deliberately step into a puddle on her way home; oh no, not she.

The teacher put a full stop after the last word she had written on the blackboard and started to explain to the children the meaning of poetry. It was a question of the endings of the words; if the children found that the endings were the same, they were confronted by poetry. The mistress gave examples: day—May, rain—pain, table—able. For the next few minutes the children had to guess the poetry that matched words given by the teacher. Helen, the model pupil, excelled herself. When the mistress called out "feet" she responded at once with "meat". Her blue eyes were shining with pleasure that the lesson was only in its first half and already she had learned something new. There was, however, some confusion caused by little Billy. In reply to the teacher's "fog", instead of producing, according to the rules, something like "dog", he announced loudly "trumpet". Everybody was surprised and the teacher scolded him, but little Billy was adamant. With a serious expression he repeated "trumpet" over and over again. He looked very funny while saying it because his hair was standing up like a brush.

Later the mistress said: "Now, children, you know what poetry is. On the blackboard I've written down a short poem by a great poet. Copy it neatly into your exercise books and when you get home learn the poem by heart."

Helen started on her task without delay. With her new nib scratching the paper, she wrote in her clean exercise book in the neatest possible fashion:

> The wind flapped loose, the wind was still,
> Shaken out dead from tree and hill:
> I had walked on at the wind's will,—
> I sat now, for the wind was still.

The lesson over, the children left school. Helen, meticulously avoiding the puddles in the street, went straight home. She kissed her Mummy and Daddy, ate her soup and meat and pudding and had her hour's rest. Then she started on her homework. She took out the exercise book and opened it. There were two poems in it. The one she had copied from the blackboard, "The wind flapped loose, the wind was still . . ." and another, that had been printed in large letters by the State Stationery Enterprise:

> Have a bath once a week
> So that you may never reek.

Which of the two was she supposed to learn by heart? Poor Helen; however hard she tried she could not remember. Both were good poems, there could be no doubt about it: "still" and "hill" in one and "week" and "reek" in the other.

In the end, because she was an orderly child who had been taught to work systematically, from left to right, she learnt "Have a bath . . ." and went for a walk with her mother.

The next day at school she was told to recite the poem. This she did with feeling, but to her great surprise and distress for the first time in her life she got no marks at all. The rest of the lesson passed uneventfully except for a slight ado with little Billy who had not learnt anything.

No one noticed that this was a decisive day in Helen's life. On that day her whole disposition underwent a profound change. On her way home she noticed a sign in a shop window: "Save your work with macaroni—buy it ready-made from Tony." "Macaroni—Tony," she repeated to herself with satisfaction while wading through puddles.

At home she took out all her exercise books and examined them carefully. In each of them she found a printed slogan, though not always in rhyme. In one of them, for instance, she found the simple injunction, "Keep this clean!" Remembering what she had learnt from her teacher she added in her childish hand, "Plant a bean!" In the evening she was running a high temperature.

How the child had changed! No longer would she obediently eat whatever was given to her. She would now order according to her fancy, one day sauce tartare, next day vol-au-vent, another day Hungarian goulash, and she was never satisfied with her food. Life with her became difficult. Every day she would go out, banging the door behind her, and visit a restaurant. Instead of going to bed early she would read until midnight either Andersen's tales or "Uncle John's Polish Stories". And when they had visitors, instead of saying politely "good morning", she would greet them with:

> We don't give credit here,
> It's lying on its bier,
> Killed by those in debt,
> Now it's mourned and wept.

Helen decided to become a poet. She kept a separate book for her verse.

> Driving with the P.M.A.
> Is the only healthy way.
> Heroes never can retreat,
> Just go forward on their feet.
> Come along, collect some scrap,
> That will put you on the map.

And many, many others.

At school they got used to her. But there was still trouble with little Billy. He never learnt anything.

29

A CITIZEN'S FATE

Let us be frank. In the remote corner of the country with which this story is concerned, they have the same weather as in the capital. Seasons follow each other, rain falls, winds blow, the sun shines exactly as in the big city. From the point of view of the climate you could not tell the one from the other. All the more surprising, even frightening, was the initiative of the authorities. In the full knowledge of the circumstances they decided to set up a meteorological station in this remote corner. It was not a big affair, just a small rectangle of ground surrounded by a white fence, with a box of instruments in the middle, standing on thin long legs.

Next to the station was the manager's house. Apart from looking after the instruments, his job consisted of writing accurate reports on the state of the weather so that, should questions be asked, the authorities would not be at a loss but have the necessary information at hand.

The manager was a most conscientious young man. He wrote his reports in a neat, legible hand and always truthfully. If it rained he would not rest until he had described the rain from every possible angle: when, how much, for how long. . . . If the sun was shining he would also spare no effort to describe it accurately. He was quite impartial. He knew that the State was working hard to get the money for his salary and he felt that he had to apply himself to his job. There was never any shortage of work because in his district there was always weather of one kind or another.

Towards the end of the summer storms became frequent and they brought rain with them. Truthfully he described them in detail and sent his reports to the head office. The storms continued.

One day he had a visit from an old and experienced colleague who, having watched him at work, remarked casually before leaving: "I wonder, my friend, if your reports aren't a bit on the depressing side."

"What do you mean?" The manager was surprised. "You can see with your own eyes that it's pouring with rain."

"Yes, yes. Of course, everybody can see that. But you do understand, don't you, that we must approach the problem consciously. Scientifically. Mind you, it's none of my business. I just mentioned it out of friendship."

The old meteorologist put on his goloshes and went away, still shaking his head. The young manager was left alone and continued compiling his reports. He gazed at the sky with some anxiety, but he went on writing.

About that time he received an unexpected summons from his higher authority. Not the highest one, but still an authority. He took his umbrella and went to the town. The authority received him in a lovely house. Rain was drumming on the roof.

"We have summoned you," announced the authority, "because we are surprised by the one-sided nature of your reports. For some time now they've been dominated by a pessimistic note. The harvest is on the way, and you keep on talking about rain. Don't you understand the responsible nature of your work?"

"But it keeps on raining . . ." said the manager.

"Don't prevaricate." The authority looked angry and his

fist landed with a bang on a pile of papers on his desk. "We have here all your recent reports. You can't deny them. You are a good worker but you are spineless. I want you to understand that we shan't tolerate any defeatism!"

After the interview the meteorologist returned to his station with the folded umbrella under his arm. In spite of this show of good will he was soaked to the skin, caught a cold and had to stay in bed. However, he would not admit that this was because of the rain.

The following day the weather improved. He was delighted and immediately wrote his report:

"The rain has stopped completely and it has to be admitted that it has never rained very much. Just a few drops now and again. But now, what sunshine!"

Indeed, the sun had broken through the clouds, it became warm and the earth was steaming. Humming gaily the manager went about his duties. In the afternoon clouds began to gather once more, driven by a cold wind. He went inside, afraid of catching 'flu. The time for his next report came and he wrote: "The sun behaves as usual. Already Copernicus has demonstrated that the setting of the sun is only apparent. In reality it always shines, only . . ."

At this point he broke off, feeling very unhappy. When the first lightning struck, he shook off his opportunism and wrote simply: "17.00 hours. Thunderstorms."

Next day brought another storm. He reported it. The day after, no storm, but hail. He reported it. A strange calm, even a feeling of satisfaction, came over him. It lasted until the postman brought him another summons. This time it was from the Central Authority.

When he returned from the capital there were no doubts in his mind. For several days running he reported bright, sunny weather. Occasionally his reports struck a dialectical

tone. For instance: "Occasional showers of short duration have caused certain flooding, but nothing can break the fighting spirit of the sappers and rescue detachments."

More reports followed with descriptions of fine weather. Some of them were even written in verse. However, some two months later he wrote a report which must have puzzled the authority. It said: "Blasted cloudburst." Underneath, hastily written in pencil, was the following sentence: "But the baby boy who was born to the widow in the village is doing well, though nobody thought he would last long."

An investigation disclosed that he had written the report while under the influence of alcohol purchased with money obtained from the sale of his meteorological instruments.

Thereafter nothing disturbed the sunny weather in his district. He was killed by lightning while walking round the fields, with a miraculous bell from Lourdes in his hand, trying to dispel the clouds. Basically he was an honest man.

30

MY UNCLE'S STORIES

Cheers. One day I was playing cards with my brother-in-law. Luck was on my side and he lost game after game. When he pushed the last of his money across the table to me, he belched and said, "It's a dog's life."

At that moment the door opened and a large St. Bernard dog came in. "What's the matter?" it asked in a deep baritone.

*   *   *

Ding dong. You wouldn't remember that Easter Sunday many, many years ago. What a festive day! The Bishop had arrived with his prelates, a crowd of people. . . . But when the bells were rung, not a sound came. I give you my word. You see, we had a few atheists in the town and they had secretly removed the bells, replacing them with felt hats. I must say, the idea wouldn't have occurred to me.

*   *   *

In principle yes. So you say, he can imitate the cuckoo. Well, there are some who can imitate and some who can't. But he can? Well, well.

*   *   *

I remember, at school, I had a friend called Charlie. He was a gay boy. Very gifted, too. Very gifted. Splendid mathematician, jolly good at moving his ears and also wonderful at imitating water. He used to sit in the front row but they had to move him to the back because all the masters were beginning to suffer from rheumatism. And one day during the physics lesson old Sieczko said, "Don't sit near the barometer, Charlie. You make it fall."

But that was nothing. Sometimes, when we asked him, Charlie would climb up to the roof and float down the gutter with a soft gurgle. That's what he was like.

*　　　*　　　*

Now, General Pulaski, that was a leader. But, you know, even today friendship isn't all that rare. The other day I was out in the street. Beastly cold. After all it's the middle of the winter. I noticed two young men walking along. Suddenly one of them turned and hit the other. . . . And they went on walking, with the first youngster hitting, and hitting, and the second one not saying a word, though his teeth were chattering. At long last, the second young man, rubbing his swollen eye, asked, "Well now, feeling warmer?"

*　　　*　　　*

Te Deum. The wedding and the reception were splendid. The bride had been given lots of presents. Among them was a six-valve radio set, the gift of Frank, her childhood friend. Everybody admired the set and without delay they plugged it in. The first sound that came out of the loudspeaker was "The Blue Danube".

The newly-weds, their parents, and all the guests eagerly sat down at a long table. The bride had her groom on her right and Frank, the young man who had given her the radio, on her left. By the time they reached the salad stage the bride's parents became very sentimental and started recalling her childhood days.

"She always was a charming child, wasn't she, Frank?"

Frank agreed. The old couple were happy and, because of

Frank's generous gift, they felt obliged to pay special attention to him. That's why they kept on talking to him.

"My goodness," sighed the mother, "what an affectionate girl she was, and so gifted. Wasn't she, Frank?"

Frank agreed.

"She was such an excellent pupil, too, so hardworking, but never averse to a bit of healthy exercise," said the mother. "I remember how overjoyed she was when we bought her a bicycle after her matriculation. And she already knew how to ride it! Frank had taught her in our back yard. It took her no time to learn. Wasn't it so, Frank?"

Frank agreed.

"Good thing—a bicycle." Her father came to life. "I remember . . ."

His wife, immersed in her memories, interrupted him. "Youth, gaiety, life, joy. Mind you, in my youth children didn't have the same advantages as you have. Sport, for instance, excursions; you just mount your bicycle and off you go to the woods. For a whole day."

"That was at Whitsun," said Frank, helping himself to more salad.

"It always rains at Whitsun," declared the bridegroom.

"On the contrary," objected his mother-in-law. "Usually it's lovely weather. Isn't that so, Frank?"

Frank agreed.

"The Blue Danube" had come to an end. The next waltz was "An Artist's Life". With satisfaction the bridegroom thought how nice it would be to listen to the radio alone with his wife, after everybody had gone.

Hence the saying: He celebrates like a bridegroom with a radio set.

*　　*　　*

One day, years ago, a cousin came to stay on my farm.

He was wearing a cassock because he was a missionary. We embraced each other. He was to spend a few days with me; for the sake of the fresh air, you know.

I asked him many questions about Africa, but he was only preparing to go there and couldn't tell me much. Gripped by curiosity I went to a second-hand bookshop and bought a volume entitled *Missionary Guide*, which described various methods. And often we would sit, my cousin and I, and read this book on the verandah until dusk came. The most interesting thing was how the Negroes like the missionaries. Of course, it takes all sorts to make a world. Some will eat a steak and be satisfied but for others there can be no dinner without a priest.

So we read and read until the light gave out, though mosquitoes kept on biting us and the evening chilled our bones. Sometimes our ardour became so great that we would stop reading and I would call to my cousin:

"Listen, Bernard, you'll convert them, won't you?"

"I shall," he would answer.

And I would embrace him and we would both be deeply moved.

In this way, slowly, I learnt everything about Africa. I knew so much about lions that you could have wakened me in the middle of the night and I'd recite it all. The jungle became as familiar as my own fields.

Often we discussed the best ways of approaching a black man so as to achieve a quick and smooth conversion. We would even hold rehearsals from time to time. I would stand in the middle of the verandah and pretend to be a Negro and Bernard would try to convert me. I must admit that he was good at it and sometimes, however much I prevaricated, he did convert me. But I was doing my best, too, and occasionally Bernard would be covered in sweat before he succeeded.

By the middle of the summer we became so expert that we decided to change rôles and Bernard in turn pretended to be a Negro. At first he did it reluctantly, but later he unwound and admitted that the exercise gave him a better insight into Negro mentality. In time I became so good at it that I could convert fifty blacks in a day, more if the weather was good.

In August we came somehow to a halt. It was all right for Bernard to spend whole days like this, but I had other things on my mind. The harvest was on, threshing . . . I neglected him somewhat during that time; I'd go into the field, he'd pick bilberries or sit on the swing in the garden. One night at dinner I mentioned that the best season for converting Negroes was in the autumn and, if one considered their culinary habits, surely one had to assume that from time to time they would be satisfied with a vegetarian meal. So, if one took some bilberries in vinegar, and some dried macaroni, if one let them try, showed them how to prepare it, maybe they'd be less keen on missionaries and healthier, too, for, come to think of it, what vitamins can there be in a missionary? Though I could ill afford it, I even offered to prepare all the provisions for Bernard's journey. But somehow time passed and Bernard stayed.

As the evenings got longer we took to playing chess. Occasionally, when he took one of my knights or bishops I'd mention that if one doesn't convert a Negro before St. Martin's Day it becomes much more difficult, because the Negroes don't like to start anything at the beginning of the year.

We started playing sixty-six, but in cards, too, Bernard had incredible luck. Looking at my miserable hand and noticing a Jack I'd say how much it resembled a Negro. "To convert a Negro like him," I said, "one has to start at the earliest possible moment. If one leaves it till later, there's never enough time, something always crops up, and there can't be anything worse than a half converted Negro."

Mind you, I was always very tactful and subtle about it, but I slipped up in October and made a reckless remark. I can't forgive myself that one word.

We were having an early dinner. Indoors, of course, because of the season. Bernard asked me to pass him the salt. And I said: "Salt is white, Negroes are black."

"What are you trying to say?" asked Bernard and stopped eating his soup. Angrily I attacked a piece of meat with my fork and said nothing.

"If I'm in your way, I shall go," said Bernard.

He got up and went out into the garden. I could see him walking down to the lake. He sat down by its edge with his back to the house. Offended. I didn't react. I finished my meal, lit my pipe and pretended that nothing had happened. I even whistled a little to improve my morale.

It was already dark and still no sign of Bernard. I got worried. Also, I was feeling sorry—after all it was Bernard. So I went out and started calling, softly at first: "Bernard!"

Silence.

"Bernard! What are you doing there? After all, you've plenty of time. The black chaps will probably convert themselves."

There was no reply. Seriously worried now, I ran to the lake. Good heavens! There was nobody there. Only the reeds were shivering above the unfathomed depth.

To this day I don't know if Bernard slipped and drowned in the mud or went to Africa.

The uncertainty is killing me.

31

THE PASTOR

Pastor Peters was a young man. He wore rimless glasses; his soft, thinning hair was parted on the left.

Until he became a missionary, he had never left San Francisco. His father had also been a pastor and, at the same time, acted as the legal adviser to his religious body. Peters senior used to deliver his sermons to a congregation of white-collar workers, looked after the legal department and had some shipping shares. Then he died just as his son was leaving the missionary college.

The superiors, who had decided to send young Peters away, had acted wisely. His average intelligence would not allow him to occupy a leading position in the Church, but it was sufficient for giving religious instruction to coloured children. They sent him to Tokyo.

He spent his journey in prayer and contemplation of his mission. His father had brought him up on strict lines and the number of prayers Peters knew was great.

In Tokyo he was told by his superiors: "You've been assigned a hard task but one that's particularly dear to Our Lord. You'll go to Hiroshima."

He remembered the name from the enormous newspaper headlines he had seen when he was sixteen years old.

When he reached Hiroshima young Pastor Peters felt sad. The city was quite unlike San Francisco.

The mission house stood among a cluster of small dwellings by the motorway.

He devoted a great deal of time and effort to the preparation of his first sermon. Though he understood nothing, Peters was unable to deliver a sermon without a thesis. For the purpose of his first public appearance in Hiroshima he formulated a double thesis: the defence of the faithful from the sins threatening them in their misery, and the parallel argument about their misery, which resulted from the war, being a punishment for their sins. As the most suitable text he chose Matthew, chapter 24.

The faithful, who numbered a few score, were recruited from the neighbourhood of the mission. The services took place once a week in the chapel, the congregation attending only for the sermon. They sat silently on their benches, and when the preacher finished they went into the courtyard where they were given some meat soup. Then they disappeared until the following Sunday.

It must be said that young Pastor Peters was nervous as he went up to the pulpit. However the familiar words of chapter 24 brought back his self-confidence. Raising his voice he read:

". . . See ye not all these things? Verily I say unto you, there shall not be left here one stone upon another, that shall not be thrown down."

He looked at the congregation. They were sitting grey and shrivelled.

". . . And ye shall hear of wars and rumours of wars; see that ye be not troubled: for all these things must come to pass, but the end is not yet.

"For nation shall rise against nation, and kingdom against kingdom: and there shall be famines, and pestilences, and earthquakes, in divers places.

"All these are the beginning of sorrows.

"Then shall they deliver you up to be afflicted, and shall kill you. . . ."

He raised his head because he could hear footsteps. A blind girl was feeling her way to the door. He was surprised and indignant but his eyes returned to the Book on the pulpit.

". . . Let him which is on the housetop not come down to take any thing out of his house:

"Neither let him which is in the field return back to take his clothes. . . ."

Others started to follow in the wake of the blind girl; they were going out into the street. In an orderly fashion they were filing out, those nearer to the door waiting till the aisle was clear, then turning and making intently for the exit. Young Pastor Peters watched them from the pulpit, his mouth wide open. But not in vain had prayer always preceded his meals for so many years; now it seemed to him that the only force which could arrest this exodus from the chapel was the Word, the Word printed in black on the pages of the Book that was lying open before him.

". . . And woe unto them that are with child, and to them that give suck in those days!

"But pray ye that your flight be not in the winter, neither on the sabbath day:

"For then shall be great tribulation, such as was not since the beginning of the world to this time, no, nor ever shall be.

"And except those days should be shortened, there should no flesh be saved. . . ."

He raised his head again and looked round with the eyes of a child whose parents, in spite of their solemn promise, refuse to take him to the cinema. The chapel was empty. Only one man remained, kneeling in front of the altar. He was an old man, his head bent down to the floor. The empty chapel shook slightly as lorries passed by and from the courtyard there came the aroma of meat soup.

He read the last quotation.

"But he that shall endure unto the end, the same shall be saved."

He closed his Bible and turned to his last listener.

The old man was swaying as if he were about to fall, but somehow regained his balance just in time. He was asleep. The war had damaged his hearing. He was deaf.

32

AN EVENT

I was sitting in an old and empty café, drinking my tea, when I noticed walking across my table a creature whom I can only describe as an elderly elf. He was a very small creature wearing a grey jacket and carrying a diminutive brief-case. I was so surprised that at first I did not know how to behave. But when I saw that he was already passing my box of cigarettes and making for the far edge of the table without paying the slightest attention to me, I called out: "Hallo!"

He stopped and looked at me without surprise. It seemed that the existence of people of my size was a matter of course to him, something that had been known and proved for a long time.

"Hallo!" I repeated clumsily. "Well . . . so you are?"

He shrugged his shoulders. I realised my lack of tact. "Yes . . . well, of course . . . it's quite natural," I added quickly, "it's quite simple." And, changing the subject, "What's the news?"

"Oh, just the same."

"Yes, quite so," I agreed cunningly. "Of course."

But somehow, in the depths of my soul, I could not get rid of the feeling that had gripped me when I first saw him, a feeling of unusualness and excitement. It was an ordinary day, I was an average man, a citizen of a country that was neither large nor very small, I was earning my living but had no prospects of making a fortune. Now that the chance had come my way to discover the deeper meaning of things I was not prepared to let it go. Having collected my wits I spoke to him artfully.

"Just the same, you say. But you know, sometimes I feel that all this banality of ordinary, unchanging life is just a pretext, just a smoke screen, hiding a wider and deeper meaning. Or at least a meaning. Perhaps we are too close to details to be able to comprehend the whole complex of things, but we can feel it."

He looked at me with indifference.

"My dear sir," he said, "I'm a simple elf. You wouldn't expect me to know about such things."

"Quite so," I agreed, "but aren't you worried by a feeling that everything is in fact different from what it appears to be, not to mention that we are surrounded by many more phenomena than we can perceive? That our small experiences are not 'it'? Have you never been tempted to push through the fog that's obscuring our true field of vision and find out what's behind it? Forgive me, if I appear to be pressing you unduly, but I seldom have an opportunity to talk to someone of your kind."

"Not at all," he answered with conventional politeness. "But, regarding what you've been saying, really one is much too busy to worry one's head about such things. One's got to live, you know."

I could not believe it. I would not forgo this conversation for anything on earth. If only thanks to the juxtaposition of the parties it gave me an opportunity for discovery, even in the empirical sense.

"I often think," I went on, catching the button of his jacket with my finger nail, "I often think that one should try to solve mysteries. Let's consider art, for instance. I feel that art is a frontier, but I can't say what it separates, I don't know what's on one side of it and what's on the other. Now imagine that art is a frontier between you and me. Where does that place art?"

"I am not an educated man," he said, trying in vain to free his button; I was fifty times his size. "For all I know, you may be right, but there are so many directions . . . There's only one thing to do—take life as it comes."

"As it comes!" I exclaimed. Here was I facing someone of whose existence I had had no notion; the very discovery of his being there was for me an enormous step forward. I had to exploit the encounter. "Look, let's not get lost in details, let's just try to get an answer to one question: what is life?"

"My dear sir," he answered patiently, "I've told you that I am a simple elf. How can you expect me to know about such things. Life just goes by, days pass one after another and each of them has to be lived somehow. After all, you are a man of experience."

"Precisely. Life goes by. I'll never believe that it just passes, that there are no disguised meanings, no false bottoms, no hidden grains of gold. Don't you agree?"

"Just look at me," said the elf, showing much less impatience than one would have expected. "Do I look as if I knew the answers? Am I a priest or a philosopher? The strangeness of life, my dear sir, that's fine in books, but it's no good to us. We can't expect manna from heaven."

"So you won't tell me, you don't want to tell me!" I was gripped by fury, perfectly understandable in the circumstances I knew that I was losing something. Disillusioned and depressed I let go of his button.

"You think it's mischief on my part." The elf sounded worried. "But I give you my word that even if our thoughts

sometimes follow your lines, it's very difficult to reach any
valid conclusions because we are surrounded by harsh and
well defined reality. And that's what counts. Don't clutter
up your head with the strange and the unusual."

"You mean it?" I asked, feeling somewhat comforted.

"I give you my word. And now, will you excuse me,
please. I must go. That's life. Au revoir."

"Au revoir."

He continued his journey across the table and disappeared
behind a bench.

33

ON A JOURNEY

Just after B—— the road took us among damp, flat meadows.
Only here and there the expanse of green was broken by a
stubble field. In spite of mud and potholes the chaise was
moving at a brisk pace. Far ahead, level with the ears of the
horses, a blue band of the forest was stretching across the
horizon. As one would expect at that time of the year, there
was not a soul in sight.

Only after we had travelled for a while did I see the first
human being. As we approached his features became clear;
he was a man with an ordinary face and he wore a Post Office
uniform. He was standing still at the side of the road, and
as we passed he threw us an indifferent glance. No sooner
had we left him behind than I noticed another one, in a similar
uniform, also standing motionless on the verge. I looked at
him carefully, but my attention was immediately attracted
by the third and then the fourth still figure by the roadside.
Their apathetic eyes were all fixed in the same direction, their
uniforms were faded.

Intrigued by this spectacle I rose in my seat so that I could
glance over the shoulders of the cabman; indeed, ahead of us
another figure was standing erect. When we passed two more
of them my curiosity became irresistible. There they were,
standing quite a distance from each other, yet near enough
to be able to see the next man, holding the same posture and

paying as much attention to us as road signs do to passing travellers. And as soon as we passed one, another came into our field of vision. I was about to open my mouth to ask the coachman about the meaning of those men, when, without turning his head, he volunteered: "On duty."

We were just passing another still figure, staring indifferently into the distance.

"How's that?" I asked.

"Well, just normal. They are standing on duty," and he urged the horses on.

The coachman showed no inclination to offer any further elucidation; perhaps he thought it was superfluous. Cracking his whip from time to time and shouting at the horses, he was driving on. Roadside brambles, shrines and solitary willow trees came to meet us and receded again in the distance; between them, at regular intervals, I could see the now familiar silhouettes.

"What sort of duty are they doing?" I enquired.

"State duty, of course. Telegraph line."

"How's that? Surely for a telegraph line you need poles and wires!"

The coachman looked at me and shrugged his shoulders.

"I can see that you've come from far away," he said. "Yes, we know that for a telegraph you need poles and wires. But this is wireless telegraph. We were supposed to have one with wires but the poles got stolen and there's no wire."

"What do you mean, no wire?"

"There simply isn't any," he said, and shouted at the horses.

Surprise silenced me for the moment but I had no intention of abandoning my enquiries.

"And how does it work without wires?"

"That's easy. The first one shouts what's needed to the second, the second repeats it to the third, the third to the fourth and so on until the telegram gets to where it's supposed to. Just now they aren't transmitting or you'd hear them yourself."

"And it works, this telegraph?"

"Why shouldn't it work? It works all right. But often the message gets twisted. It's worst, when one of them has had a drink too many. Then his imagination gets to work and various words get added. But otherwise it's even better than the usual telegraph with poles and wires. After all live men are more intelligent, you know. And there's no storm damage to repair and great saving on timber, and timber is short. Only in the winter there are sometimes interruptions. Wolves. But that can't be helped."

"And those men, are they satisfied?" I asked.

"Why not? The work isn't very hard, only they've got to

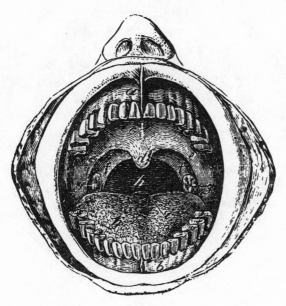

know foreign words. And it'll get better still; the postmaster has gone to Warsaw to ask for megaphones for them so that they don't have to shout so much."

"And should one of them be hard of hearing?"

"Ah, they don't take such-like. Nor do they take men with a lisp. Once they took on a chap that stammered. He got his job through influence but he didn't keep it long because he was blocking the line. I hear that by the twenty kilometres' stone there's one who went to a drama school. He shouts most clearly."

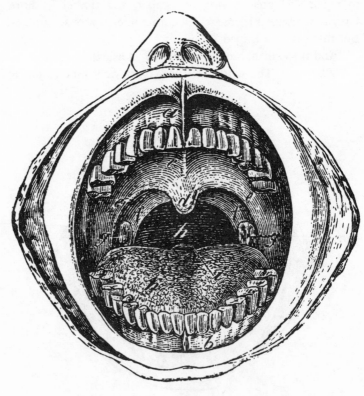

His arguments confused me for a while. Deep in thought, I no longer paid attention to the men by the road verge. The chaise was jumping over potholes, moving towards the forest, which was now occupying most of the horizon.

"All right," I said carefully, "but wouldn't you prefer to have a new telegraph with poles and wires?"

"Good heavens, no." The coachman was shocked. "For the first time it's easy to get a job in our district in the telegraph, that is. And people don't have to rely only on their wages either. If someone expects a cable and is particularly anxious not to have it twisted, then he takes his chaise along the line and slips something into the pocket of each one of the telegraph boys. After all a wireless telegraph is something different from one with wires. More modern."

Over the rattle of the wheels I could hear a distant sound, neither a cry nor a shout, but a sort of sustained wailing.

"Aaaeeeaaauuueeeaaaeeeaayayay."

The coachman turned in his seat and put his hand to his ear.

"They are transmitting," he said. "Let's stop so that we can hear better."

When the monotonous noise of our wheels ceased, total silence enveloped the fields. In that silence the wailing, which resembled the cry of birds on a moor, came nearer to us. His hand cupped to his ear, the telegraph man near by made ready to receive.

"It'll get here in a moment," whispered the coachman.

Indeed. When the last distant "ayayay" died away, from behind a clump of trees came the prolonged shout:

"Fa ... th ... er dea ... d fu ... ner ... al Wed ... nes- ... day."

"May he rest in peace," sighed the coachman and cracked his whip. We were entering the forest.

34

ART

"Art educates. That's why writers must know life. Proust is the best example. He knew nothing about life. He cut himself off; he shut himself up in a cork-lined room. An extreme case. One can't write in cork-lined rooms. One can't hear anything. And what are you writing now?"

"It's a story for a competition. I've already worked out the idea. It's about a remote village which is changing very slowly and with difficulty. Little Johnny is a cowhand in the service of a rich peasant. While in the fields he suddenly hears the hum of engines. It's a steel bird, a plane. Johnny looks up and dreams of becoming a pilot. And then—oh wonder—the plane comes lower and lower and lands on the meadow. A figure clad in a flying suit and goggles jumps out of the cockpit. Johnny runs towards him as fast as his legs will go. The stranger smiles at the panting boy and enquires about the nearest smithy. Some small part needs repairing. Johnny brings help. When the repair is completed, the pilot thanks Johnny, and, noticing his eyes shining with curiosity and enthusiasm, says: 'You'd like to fly yourself, wouldn't you?' The boy, struck dumb by excitement, can only nod his head. The engine starts and soon the plane is flying over the meadow. The pilot leans from the cockpit and waves Johnny goodbye.

"Time passes. Johnny continues to look after the cows. But he can't forget the incident with the pilot. At last one day the postman approaches the cabin where Johnny lives with his widowed mother. From far away he's waving a white envelope and there is a smile on his face. An invitation to a school for airmen: the pilot hasn't forgotten his promise. Johnny is beside himself with joy.

"He goes to the city and joins the school. When he has finished his training he is given a plane. In a few seconds his steel bird is airborne. Johnny's mother comes out of the cabin and, shading her eyes with her hand, looks to the sky. Johnny circles the village and waves to his mother. His dream has come true."

"Yes, indeed. If the writer knows life, his work is often progressive, even though his own consciousness may lag behind. Balzac is a typical example. He had a tendency to eulogise the aristocracy and the monarchy, but his realistic work points in the opposite direction. I think I've read your story in the last issue of——"

"Yes. 'Frank's Adventure'. That was commissioned. It was a question of illustrating a typical problem of psychology concerning the life of youth. A group of boys goes on an excursion. They sing as they march long. They all keep together, except Frank who leaves the party surreptitiously. He rejects his colleagues and wants to cross the forest by himself. Soon he loses his way and falls into a pit. He tries to climb out, but he can't. In the end he cries for help. His colleagues come to the rescue and, amid jokes and jeers, extricate him from the pit. After this experience Frank never separates himself from his colleagues."

"Yes. Art has a noble task: to educate man. That's why the writer's part in our society is a most responsible one. The writers are the architects of human souls and the critics are the architects of the writers' souls. Can you, by any chance, lend me five hundred zlotys?"

"I'm afraid that three hundred is all I can manage."

"All right, three hundred will do."

35

A FORESTER IN LOVE

Once upon a time there was a forester who had an exceptionally large moustache. The moustache was the pride of his
life. He looked splendid with it.

The forester was in love with a young lady who lived in
the nearby mansion. To find an excuse for going to the mansion he used to shoot hares and take them to the big house.
Even then he did not see her every time because often she was
reading in the library or raiding the larder.

The hares were often out of favour with the family and its
guests and the young lady's mother would say, looking fixedly
at her daughter: "Those hares, again."

On these occasions the young lady would blush and drop
her head.

The forester was shy. And in any case the difference between
their social positions would not allow him to come near his
beloved.

But once it seemed as if his prayers were about to be
answered.

He had just shot a hare and was bringing it to the mansion.
Instead of approaching from the back, he came from the
side, through the gardens. He saw the young lady sitting in a
summer-house. Alone. Her hands were resting on an open
book. She was day-dreaming about something. A lock of hair
had fallen on her forehead, her mouth was slightly open and
her breasts were rising and falling with her fast breathing.

The forester was enraptured by this sight. He was ready to drop the hare, jump over the fence separating them, fall on his knees and confess his love for her.

At that very moment, however, the lady of the house emerged from the kitchen quarters followed by a maid carrying a basket of washing. The lady liked to see to everything herself, and when it was pointed out to her that she was tiring herself out, she always answered: "If you don't keep a pond clean it gets full of frogs—without me the household will go to the dogs."

She looked around and noticed that the clothes-lines were not there; they had been left in the shed.

"Come and stand here for a moment," she said to the forester and tied one end of his enormous moustache to one tree and the other end to a second tree.

"I must get this washing dry," she explained. "It's clouding over and it might start raining soon. My husband will see that you are paid for it."

She ordered the maid to hang the washing on the stretched moustache of the forester. The servant did as she was told and then went away taking the empty basket with her.

The forester was left alone, his moustache tied to two trees. In one hand he was still holding the hare.

How could he approach his beloved in these circumstances?

She was still sitting in the summer-house, staring into the distance as if she had noticed something indefinable between heaven and earth, something unknown to other people but discernible to the heart of a young woman.

The forester stood still like a statue. He would have gladly given a tug to his moustache to get free but he was afraid even to breathe, lest his beloved should notice him. It was not so much that he was ashamed at having been made to perform an unmanly function. He would have suffered gladly in return for just one look from her. But this washing . . . it was hers. He was so embarrassed, so afraid that she would glance at him, so anxious not to make a noise that he stood on tip-toe. The blush on his face was becoming deeper and deeper, hotter and hotter, until his tears started to sizzle on his burning cheeks.

The young lady slowly shut her book. She rose. She floated across the lawn towards the pond and she started feeding the swans. Her eyes were still the same, remote, dreaming. Had she noticed the fate of the unfortunate forester? We do not know. Who can read a woman's heart?

And the forester? He was seen a few days later selling hares at a market. His moustache had been cut short. It did not suit him. Girls were laughing at him.

36

SPRING IN POLAND

That year April was exceptionally warm. Early in the month, just before noon one day, the crowds milling on the pavements of the main Warsaw thoroughfares witnessed a most unusual happening. Floating above the rooftops like a bird was a man. He was dressed in an ordinary grey raincoat and hat; under his arm a brief-case. He was not using any mechanical aids but slight movements of his hands and arms were enough to keep him flying.

The man circled above the building of the International Press Club and then, as if having noticed something in the road, he dived. Astonished passers-by stopped dead. He was now flying so low that they could see the glint of the ring on his finger and examine the condition of the soles of his shoes. With a loud and penetrating wail the man soared again, circled majestically above the city centre, and flew away in a southerly direction.

It is fully understandable that the event gave rise to a great deal of talk. The news was withheld from the press and radio because the political attitude of the bird-man was not known, but all the same the whole country was soon aware of the strange occurrence. There can be no doubt that this happening would have been long remembered were its memory not erased by further and even stranger developments which took place a few days later: two other men, also with brief-cases, were observed flying through the clouds above the centre of Warsaw. They too disappeared in a southerly direction.

The advance of the spring brought in its wake even warmer weather. Above Warsaw, later also above the provincial cities and even above the smaller district towns, the sight of men with brief-cases flying in twos and threes, but more often singly, became a daily occurrence. They all floated gracefully and performed aerobatics, but in the end they always flew away towards the south.

The nation demanded to be told the truth. There seemed to be no point in trying to hush it all up, and a communiqué was issued, announcing that, as the result of rising temperatures during the mild spring weather and the opening of windows in Government offices, many civil servants, yielding to their eagle nature, had been leaving their desks and flying out of the windows. The communiqué ended with an appeal to civil servants and all other Government employees to remember the lofty aims of the five-year plan, to conquer the urge of their blood and to remain at their posts. During the following days mass meetings of civil servants were held at which they gave pledges to fight their nature and not to fly away. This led to tragic conflicts. In spite of their will to stay, the numbers flying above the capital and other cities did not diminish. They could be observed diving in and out of white cumulus clouds, turning somersaults in the blue skies, wallowing in sunsets and, drunk with the power of flying, racing ahead of spring storms. Sometimes they would come down almost to ground level only to soar again to a height which made them invisible. In the streets passers-by found spectacles, spats and scarves raining from the sky, lost in the mad flight. In the emptying offices work was grinding to a halt.

From the Tatra mountains in the south came alarming reports. The mountain guards had observed masses of civil

servants settling on crests and peaks, flying about and causing damage to the wild life of the national park. Complaints from the population started coming in thick and fast. In the Nowy Targ district twenty-eight lambs disappeared without trace, and at Muszyna an eagle, which was later identified as the deputy director of a Government department, made a particularly daring raid and flew away with a pig. They descended from the skies like lightning.

May was on the way, and in all the offices windows were wide open. The situation was made even more serious by the fact that most cases of reversal to eagles took place among the central authorities. In fact, the higher the authority the larger the percentage of officials turning into birds of prey. All this adversely affected the reputation of the State, especially that again and again people saw high officials, known to them only from photographs and public appearances, floating above their heads, waving their legs and turning like balloons.

A decree was issued ordering windows in all public offices and institutions to be kept shut—in vain. The windows remained closed, but a true eagle can escape even through a small skylight.

Various other measures were tried. Lead weights attached to the shoes of civil servants proved of no avail—they escaped in their socks. Those suspected of wanting to fly away were tied to their desks with ropes but they always managed to undo the knots. And so, now and again, a civil servant would sigh, struggle for a few minutes with his sense of duty, allow his true nature to assert itself, climb the window-sill, give an embarrassed cough and fly away, often finishing his sandwiches and tea while already airborne.

In these circumstances the execution of any form of official business became very complicated indeed. The escaping civil servants usually took with them all the papers on which they had been working. I managed to get one matter settled only because a friendly forester had informed me that he had seen the official concerned fighting with a mountain goat near a well-known lake in the Tatras. Some people organised expeditions into the mountain regions where they expected to find the nests or hunting grounds of the officials dealing with their applications. In this way mountaineering flourished, but the administration of the country was disorganised.

The foresters and mountain guards were issued with new orders: they were to catch the fugitive officials. But who can catch a bird that flies like an arrow! Only one method produced surprisingly good results: nets around the offices of cashiers on pay day. On that day whole flocks of flying civil servants, driven by an instinct stronger than their will, circled above the pay offices, pressing against each other and issuing excited shrieks. But pay day over, they disappeared again, and those who had been caught either wasted away or escaped once more.

In this manner the spring passed, followed by a hot summer, bursting with freedom, soaring with frequent flight. Then imperceptibly, like a sickness, autumn appeared and damped down the fire of the sun. Finding food in the mountains became difficult. The day came when a party of schoolchildren on an excursion to a mountain peak saw in a crevasse a senior civil servant who did not fly away on their approach, but stood there dejectedly looking at them. His beard was hidden under the collar of his tattered coat in which he had flown away in the spring. Only when the children were almost next to him did he clumsily run a few steps and with a hoarse cry fly heavily away into the mist.

The first snow came. Its damp flakes fell silently on peasant roofs up and down the country. Under those roofs a folk song could be heard, a song full of wonder. A song about various officials, those leaders of ours—true eagles.

37

SIESTA

From the street you can only see a large building. If we pass through the hall to the back of the house we find ourselves in a small courtyard, empty and quiet. A low stone wall separates it from what must be a garden or an orchard, for we can see the green domes of trees speckled with the red of ripening cherries. As we follow the wall we come to a wooden gate made of planks grey with age. There is an iron handle on the gate, but the bolt on the other side is firm. Over the gate we can see into the garden. There is a small house built at right angles to the wall. It has a red tile roof, and a loggia in front with four arches supported by three columns. Under the arches we can see the windows of the official quarters. In the shade of the loggia two men are sitting by a table covered with a white cloth. The air is full of the smell of sandstone and warm herbs.

One of the men must be about fifty. He is bald and has a soft mouth. His navy suit is very well cut, and under his fat chin sits an immaculate, silvery bow-tie, adorning a snow-white shirt front. The other—a priest in a black cassock with a row of small buttons from top to bottom. Between them— three dark green bottles and two glasses half full of beer. On this summer Saturday afternoon they are obviously both resting from their week of toil, and with pleasure anticipating the approach of Sunday. Lazily they gaze across the garden at the towering four storeys of the now deserted Government building.

"We've known each other for so long," the priest broke the silence and reached slowly for his glass, "and yet I have no idea how I should address you."

"I quite understand your being at a loss, Father," answered the layman. "To address me by my proper title would be quite out of place. No, I don't have in mind just, shall we say, administrative reasons. It's really a question of style. I do appreciate and respect the discretion which makes us both avoid the disharmony that would inevitably follow your making use of your knowledge of heraldry."

Priest: "On the other hand it's difficult to address you in the way accepted by your . . . That is, I wanted to say . . ."

The priest blushed. He coughed to hide his confusion.

"My employers?" said the man. "By all means let's call a spade a spade. I am indeed a paid employee and I'm not restricted by the severe discipline of that order. What's more, my value as an employee consists also in preserving in an unadulterated and fresh condition some of the principles that bind our mutual—— How shall I put it?"

It was his turn to hum and haw and show slight embarrassment.

The priest hastened to interject: "Let's call them opinion formers. And, taking a broader view, our fellow men. Yes, opinion formers or fellow men. Fellow men, who——"

"I understand. I understand and I feel that we needn't search for a more precise definition. But since we've broached the subject. I too must admit to having been worried by some doubts. For instance, to this day I'm not sure if it would be proper to address you as, shall we say, chaplain?"

"Chaplain?"

"Yes. As far as I know that's how one describes a priest

who performs his duties in connection with, or within the framework of, a lay institution, the army, a prison, or . . ."

"May I point out that in this particular case we are dealing with an institution that's more than lay."

"Quite so. Please forgive my importunity. More than lay. Indeed. You do appreciate, Father, don't you, that should your presence here and occupation become generally known, the surprise of people would be quite natural and understandable?"

"The same would happen in your case."

"Yes, but not quite to the same degree. After all my work doesn't reach into the regions of the soul, into philosophy. I'm saying it also to underline my respect for the subtle task of any priest, for the realm of faith and art and thought. As for me, when we have a visit from an eminent member of the Control Council, from an artist or a king I go to greet him because from childhood I've known what food should be served, what wine and in what glasses, I speak a few languages, I know the history of art and I'm not a Communist. The work is quite hard but it isn't monotonous because in between those visits I teach the young how to dance. I teach the sons and daughters of the Secretaries of the Councils. My duties are clearly defined and, conversation apart, they don't exceed purely physical activities·"

"Well, well. Is that all?"

"No, you're quite right. I also remind them of the dates and organize the celebrations of the more important anniversaries which, being alien to the strict outlook of our superiors, have, however, a certain appeal among some sections of the population. That's why they are loyally observed. But all this is delegated work which doesn't come within the strict terms of reference of my official duties. Now, as for my title it would be simplest if you called me *maître de danse*."

The priest sighed and gazed at the garden. The deep blue, spreading across the sky, heralded the approaching sunset. Everything was still and quiet, remote from the hubbub of the town.

After a while he said: "You know, you've been lucky."

"I beg your pardon?" The *maître de danse* was surprised and his right hand, which held the glass, halted half-way between the table and his lips.

"I'm sorry."

Maître de danse: "Not at all. The new reality."

Priest: "The new fighting the old."

Maître de danse: "You surprise me, Padre. And it's the second time. The first time was—please forgive me—when I saw a priest here, when we met on the same official platform."

Priest: "I can see no reason for surprise. Simply, I was approached. The secretary put the matter quite openly. 'We have,' he said, 'some decent comrades, I stress some, not all, who have the fault that, begging your pardon, Padre, they do go to church. The masses see them in church and that's bad, from the tactical point of view. To expel them would break the unity of our ranks. Expulsion is no solution, but education is. On the other hand to allow a public scandal is also inadvisable, if only because of the higher authorities. That's why we have a proposition to make to you, Padre. Here, in our Committee building, we'll organise a chapel, not a large one, twenty-five feet by twenty, with one small altar. Those of our comrades who feel that they must, can worship there quietly, among themselves. In return, you, Padre, can give such sermons as you like, you can speak your mind freely be it about the Government or about Marx. It won't matter. You'll be speaking to our hardened comrades and you won't convince them. In this way we'll keep our ranks intact and people will stop talking.' That's what he told me. I accepted the job."

Maître de danse: "But . . ."

Priest: "I anticipate your arguments and your reservations. I accepted because I was relying on my sermons. There was a missionary element in my decision. Alas, the Lord punishes pride and over-confidence."

Maître de danse: "But your expression about the new and the old . . ."

Priest: "Precisely."

Maître de danse: "Is it possible that your heroic decision to enter the lion's den did not bring the desired effect?"

Priest: "My dear sir. A moment ago you spoke of the realm of soul and philosophy. You said that it was within my competence. I hope you were right. Anyhow, allow me to enter that realm for a moment. The concept of the new fighting the old is by no means in conflict with my calling and my work of a shepherd of souls. But it does express my views, which, I believe, would astound you, if our conversation exceeded the limits of an ordinary social chat between two colleagues."

Maître de danse: "I don't quite follow you."

Priest: "I am a Marxist."

The *maître de danse* raised his eyebrows, opened his mouth and arranged his lips in a circle. The priest folded his hands and looked at the sky. The *maître de danse* shut his mouth and opened it again, formulating a sentence.

"I admire you, Padre. Not departing for a moment from the fact that fine points of spiritual matters are professionally no concern of mine, I assume that ignorance and inferiority not only allow me, but they give me the right, to ask: how do you do it, Padre?"

Priest: "First of all, let me dismiss most firmly any notion of yours that my status, symbolised by this cassock, has lost any of its authenticity. On the contrary. My Marxist views have in no way weakened my priestly calling; they have strengthened it, they have added to it the lustre of a special duty, I might even say, a Party duty."

The *maître de danse* lowered his head and said in a tired voice: "I give up. Please don't regard me as an opponent in a discussion. All I want, if this is at all possible, is a simple and a patient explanation, like a child who can't understand the complexities of Catechism even though they appear to be simple and easily comprehensible to the Fathers of the Church."

Priest: "The humility of a simple believer faced by the mysteries of dogma is both appropriate and laudable. But that which surprised you at first will soon probably appear to you in clearer and simpler light. You know very well that, as an employee of the Committee, I have to attend ideological training sessions at which I've also noticed your presence."

Maître de danse: "Official necessity, nothing more. . . ."

Priest: "At first I also regarded those lectures as . . . sad reality. But soon I became interested in the theses and arguments put forward by the lecturers. Later, their logic began to convince me, in the same way in which it has convinced one quarter of all humanity—that, if I'm not mistaken, is the estimated strength of the forces of progress and democracy."

Maître de danse: "So, after all, you do admit apostasy, Padre!"

"Nothing of the sort," shouted the priest, banging the table with his hand. "Don't interrupt me, please. And no imputations . . ."

Maître de dance: "Sorry, Padre. I was carried away."

Priest: "I forgive you. I forgive you all the easier because at a certain stage of my ideological development I made exactly the same mistake as you have just made. I, too, thought for a time that I was an apostate. What's more, after a prolonged internal struggle, I decided to break with my old outlook. I went to see the Secretary and explained to him openly that, as the result of my evolution towards Marxism, I could no longer perform the functions you were pleased to describe as those of Chaplain to the Committee. The Secretary was delighted and congratulated me on my development but soon he became worried and rubbed his forehead for a long time. At last he said pensively: 'Listen, Comrade. These are no simple matters. If you stop performing your function our comrades will again have to go to church and this may cause incalculable ideological harm. Enemy propaganda will once more have something to talk about to the masses; and in everything we do we must aim at the masses. I'm delighted with the increase of your consciousness, but don't forget that this development also places new duties on you. To put it briefly, you must continue with your work here. You are one of us and you know the ground.'

"I protested. I said that the Secretary clearly did not appreciate how far my materialistic outlook had developed. It had developed to a point which made it impossible for me to carry on with my duties. The Secretary was adamant. 'On the contrary,' he said. 'It's precisely because I see that you are a truly mature person, that I rely on your understanding of tactics. Don't forget the dialectic! I know how difficult it'll be for you to remain a priest, but, banking on your high ideological development, I expect you to be able to make the sacrifice. What's more, you must realise that not only is it necessary for you to stay at your post but you have to work at it with even greater conviction to an even greater effect. You mustn't lose any of your high professional qualifications. Otherwise our comrades, having noticed a falling off in your form, may become dissatisfied and start going to church elsewhere, outside the range of our direct influence. Just think of this responsibility and you'll understand how highly I value your devotion, consciousness and fighting spirit. I appeal to your conscience.'

"After some reflection and, I must admit it, not without hesitation, I came to the conclusion that I couldn't deny the superior truth of the Secretary's reasoning. There are higher and lower causes. The higher ones can be understood only because of specific personal attitudes. A higher cause, that's what it is. Do you understand now that my calling and my outlook not only are not in conflict with each other, but they strengthen each other and together form one dialectic whole?"

The *maître de danse* wiped his face with a fine linen handkerchief and said: "Please go on."

Priest: "Yes, yes. I too had to pass through the two stages of development. First, the stage of limited horizons with a naïve and honest, ideologically critical attitude, followed by the stage of enlarged consciousness, of tactical approach, a stage that demands many sacrifices but gives you a deep feeling of severe responsibility, of strength and of usefulness to the complex apparatus, and political thought."

Maître de danse: "The sun is setting."

Priest: "Indeed. Nature is governed by its laws."

Peace and warmth radiated from the garden after long exposure to the rays of the sun. The *maître de danse* opened the third bottle and filled the glasses which were soon topped with white fringes.

"All the same," he said as he raised his glass, "I'm glad that my work, incomparably more modest, does not involve any philosophical principles. *Trois, quatre, en avant!* That's all they ask of me."

At that moment they heard someone knocking on the gate. The priest and the *maître de danse* looked at each other.

"I wonder what that can be," said the priest.

38

MODERN LIFE

Being a loyal citizen I have decided to spend one whole day entirely in the spirit and letter of official exhortations.

First Day

I administered myself a sharp blow on the head thus fighting for the underfulfilment of my quota of sleep. A few more blows, which brought me down to the floor where I held myself in a powerful "Nelson" grip, took care of further attempts at resistance.

The process of getting dressed proceeded smoothly apart from a few minor skirmishes. In this way the battle of getting up was won.

Next I directed my steps to the bathroom which soon began to reverberate with machine-gun fire; armed with a Sten gun I was fighting for the cleanliness of my teeth. I must have won this battle, too, because I soon emerged from the bathroom wearing a happy smile on my face. The rest was simply a matter of a few more shots. Stepping over the dead body of the caretaker I went out into the street.

Breakfast. In the milk bar I had to use a torpedo. This modern weapon, fired with silent accuracy, brought my victory in the battle for scrambled eggs. The girl cashier was easily defeated on points.

The rest of the day was also full of fighting for various things. The battle for putting my hat on was fought and won with side arms. Two hand grenades were needed to bring my engagement in the public convenience to an end. My purchase of cigarettes was achieved from the turret of my tank only after half an hour's fighting and the destruction of the tobacco kiosk with a direct hit.

At last, having fought for everything, having won all the battles and hoping to win all the future ones, I returned home. During a slight skirmish about retiring to bed I wounded myself with a sabre, but at last I went to sleep in a happy but strangely exhausted condition.

Second Day

This morning, when I looked out of my window, I saw a problem standing outside the door of the house. When I went out, it was still standing there in exactly the same posture as before. In the afternoon I found it as I had left it. Only in the evening did it shift its weight from one foot to the other.

I could barely sleep, worrying about the poor problem. The next morning it was still there, its posture unchanged. I brought it a folding chair so that it could rest for a while. No, it would not sit down, but from time to time it performed a knee-bending exercise. What a problem, I thought.

Every few minutes the inhabitants of the house interrupted whatever they were doing and looked out of the window to see if the problem was still there. They were getting used to it. Mothers would give it as an example to their children, men were regarding it with envy.

You can imagine the commotion there was when one morning we found the problem lying on the pavement. It did not suffer long. The Committee of Tenants paid for a decent burial. By the graveside we listened to a speech by the leader who had posed the problem outside our door. In the course of his oration he raised several new problems.

But the Committee of Tenants has no more funds for funerals.

39

THE VETERAN

Next to me, on the same landing, lived a vigorous old man. As I passed his door I could often hear him singing "When reveille calls us to the walls", "Grenadier's fate", or "Hail girls, we're coming, we're coming". I used to meet him at the small dairy where we both bought our bread, butter, milk and pickled cucumbers. He must have been over seventy but he kept his head and shoulders straight.

During the late autumn I got to know him better. One night, as I was leaving my digs and locking the door, he came out on to the landing and invited me inside for a little chat. I found myself in a cold, almost empty room with only a table, a chair, an iron bedstead and an enormous cupboard of dark, carved oak. Outside the wind rattled the black window panes pensively.

For a while we stood facing each other in silence. Then, looking me straight into the eyes, he said slowly and with emphasis:

"I was the standard bearer of the 5th Regiment."

"Yes," I said.

"Yes, of the 5th Regiment," he repeated.

We continued facing each other until, realising that his words made no impression on me, he lowered his eyes. I knew nothing about the 5th Regiment.

"Today is the regimental anniversary. It was the most

famous regiment in the whole country. But you're too young to remember."

I spread my hands in a gesture of helplessness.

"It fought well?" I asked, to please him.

"It marched! Oh, how we marched! You should have seen us marching past. That was a sight! But today . . . I've checked. There's no-one left, but me. I am the last soldier of the 5th Regiment."

"Well?"

"Today is the regimental anniversary. On this day there has always been a great march past about which the newspapers wrote at length. Our regiment was the bodyguard of the Commander-in-Chief. I was a professional. Nobody could shout as loudly as I: 'Hip, hip, hurrah!' and 'Three cheers!' "

He stood to attention, placing his hands along the seams of his trousers that were too large for him, and looked at the window with an expression of a dusty stuffed hawk.

"Excuse me," I said, "but 'three cheers' for whom?"

"Hip, hip, hurrah!"

A new gust of rain hit the windows like an echo of cheers.

He went to the cupboard. Its doors, covered with carved bunches of grapes, opened with a loud squeak. I looked over his shoulder. The only object inside the cupboard was a wooden staff wrapped in a canvas. The old man clicked his heels, gripped the staff and took it out. Regimental colours. In the dim light of a bulb suspended high under the dirty ceiling he unfolded the mouldering cloth. A golden lion was holding in its mouth the figure 5. The dark purple of the background looked warm against the flaking, naked walls of the room.

"Let's go," he said.

"Go? Where?"

He rested the colours against the cupboard and folded his hands as if in prayer.

"I implore you," he said. "Don't refuse me. It isn't far. . . . Please. . . ."

I could not refuse. He wrapped the colours in newspaper and took it outside. I followed him.

The last tram brought us to the Central Square. Rain kept on coming in squalls. We alighted. In front of us spread a vast expanse of black asphalt. The reflections of many lamps rocked by the wind were skating on the glistening surface. This used to be the venue of all parades, processions, and demonstrations. The old man was still explaining: ". . . Ours was a special regiment, for State occasions . . . we had the biggest brass band in the country. What a band!"

In turn propelled and pushed back by the gusts of wind we made our way to the centre of the square. There was no stand.

"Will you stand there," he pointed to the top of an indistinct shape near by. It was a metal rubbish bin. I climbed on to it, buttoning up my coat in an attempt to keep out the wind. Below me I could see the silhouette of the standard bearer with the colours still wrapped round the staff, like a lance.

"Let's begin," he called, and his voice had a happy tremor. "Thanks to you I'll be able to march past once more. This may well be my last march past."

"Oh, come. There's no reason to talk like that," I said politely. The wind was terrible.

He stood to attention and sharply gave the order: "Fall in!"

He went away.

I felt ridiculous precariously balancing on top of a tall rubbish bin, alone in the centre of the empty square.

Suddenly from the left the wind brought a distant voice, like a whisper: "Left, right, left, right, left . . ."

The standard-bearer appeared in the uncertain light of the street lamps. Above his head the colours were fluttering in the wind, tugging at the staff held by weak and uncertain hands.

He was approaching. Parade step. His clumsy feet rising burlesque-like and hitting the pavement with the gentlest of thuds.

"Hip, hip, hurrah!"

The wind was carrying away the old man's voice, blowing it into the corners of the enormous square.

"Hip, hip, hurrah!"

When he was only a few steps from me, he raised his head and shouted in a falsetto voice: "Eyes Riiiight!"

He passed me three times, on each occasion dipping the colours with the golden lion holding the figure 5.

With one hand I was clutching my coat. The other went slowly up to my head. I saluted.

40

THE SCEPTIC

So you say that there are people on other planets? Perhaps there are; after all they must be somewhere. But, frankly, I don't believe it. I've read a book about astronomy. Now, look how it's raining today. Without end. And now take those nebulae and balls of fire. How could man survive in those circumstances? No. It isn't possible.

Canals on Mars? Agreed. Only intelligent beings could have built them. And we know, of course, that by intelligent beings we don't mean cats or dogs, but humans. On the other hand has anyone seen them? And anyway, is it true?

It would be a good thing to have a barrel under the gutter to catch all that rainwater. Pity to let it go to waste.

Another thing; the scientists have stronger arguments; the whole world is made of the same matter. They can turn a man into a motor-cycle or lipstick. Now, that's a more serious matter. If we can have motor-cycles and lipstick here on earth, they can also exist elsewhere. But it doesn't follow that there are men on other planets.

I wonder if it will clear up today? We had such a lovely sunset last night.

Flying saucers? Yes, I've heard of them. But there's no proof, absolutely no proof.

I think it's clearing up.

What? Really? No, I didn't know. So it's a fact?

Well, well. . . . So there are intelligent beings on other planets. . . .

Well, well, well.

And what are they there for?

41

I WANT TO BE A HORSE

How I should like to be a horse. . . .

If only, looking in the glass, I could see that instead of feet and hands I had hooves, a tail at the back and an authentic horse's head, I should go straight to the housing department. . . .

"I want a large modern flat," I should say.

"You must fill in an application form and await your turn."

"Ha, ha," I would laugh. "Can't you see, gentlemen, that I'm no ordinary man-in-the-street? I'm different, I'm special."

Right away they would give me a large, modern flat with a bathroom.

I should perform in a revue and nobody would dare to say that I had no talent—even if my script was no good. On the contrary, they would praise me.

"Isn't he wonderful, for a horse," they would say.

"What a head!" others would comment.

Then there would be all the fun of sayings and proverbs: "Horse sense", "Don't look a gift horse in the mouth", "A kingdom for a horse", "A dark horse" . . .

I should attract the interest of women. "You're so different," they would say.

And when the time came for me to go to Heaven I should naturally get a pair of wings. I should become a Pegasus. A winged horse! Can there be a more beautiful fate for a man?

42

THE CHRONICLE OF A BESIEGED CITY

The city is under siege. Peasants cannot bring their produce in and prices of milk, butter and eggs have rocketed. There is a cannon in front of the Town Hall. Municipal commissionaires are dusting the cannon carefully by means of hares' legs and feather dusters. Someone advises wiping it with a wet rag. But who will listen to advice amidst the turmoil of the siege? Everyone who, hastening through the city centre, notices this cannon, finds his heart gripped by anxiety. Some people shrug their shoulders: people don't clean their shoes, and here . . . But afraid of informers they pretend that their backs are itching and they scratch between their shoulder blades. They try to make their behaviour appear to be of no importance.

As for myself, I don't regret anything. The limitations of my fate have tied me to my pokey room, they have tied me to this city and I know that I am not a Count and never shall become a Field-Marshal. The old chap who lives at the bottom of the stairs is absolutely delighted. All his life he has considered himself as a first-class shot. Now he will be able to show them. Since the morning he has been polishing his metal-rimmed glasses. He suffers from conjunctivitis.

In the afternoon a shell fell through the open door of a suburban house and killed two goldfish in an aquarium. A state funeral was ordered for them. Through the night, candles were burning around the black catafalque in the Cathedral. On the catafalque rested a coffin and in it the two goldfish; one had to look close to see them at all, lying at the bottom of the black box, as if down a precipice. Later the six horses harnessed to the hearse, feeling the lightness of their load, kept on running away. The man from the Town Hall, who was in charge of the funeral, tried to explain to them that for the good of the city they should move slowly and with dignity. The grooms surreptitiously gave them a beating, but this was also in vain.

The Archbishop, standing in front of the open grave, delivered a fiery oration, but he tripped on his robe and fell in. They buried him by mistake because nobody had noticed his fall, even though all the faces seemed full of concentration. However, he was soon unearthed and the grave-diggers had to apologise to him. He was in a sufficiently bad mood. In spite of all this, the general hatred of the enemy increased appreciably after the funeral.

That evening the old man shot the attendant who goes round at dusk and lights the gas lamps. He blamed the poor light, because, he said, he had been aiming straight at the enemy. He swore that his conjunctivitis would soon pass.

During the night there was a loud noise in the cellar of our house. Bottles of fermenting wine were exploding. We placed a guard there.

When the noise brought us all running into the cellar, I noticed that my neighbour on the landing was wearing a night-dress in a pattern resembling small autumn leaves. I mentioned it to her. It immediately brought autumn into our minds and made us feel so sad that, though everybody else went back to sleep, the two of us sat on the back steps leading into the garden and talked about that unpleasant season. Then I remembered that I had an eiderdown in a pattern of gay spring flowers. I brought it down and wrapped it round my neighbour. At once we both felt more cheerful.

In the morning—sensation. One of the patriots found a torpedo in his breakfast coffee. He reported it at once. The coffee was poured away. We now have an instruction to drink coffee only through a straw. Especially that all yoghourt has been mined. It is said that these are, in fact, our own counter-mines.

The newspaper calls for increased efforts. It appeals for deeds that will bring glory and promotion. "A General in every house" is the slogan of the day. I increased my efforts and stretched my muscles; my braces gave way. My landlady keeps on grumbling: "What do I want a General for. He won't wipe his feet, he won't even take off his hat. . . ." In a shop window, three streets away from us, they are showing a model General. I heard that one can also get herrings there. But I can't go out because of my braces.

I tried to read, but opposite my window the old boy took up his position, the one who is so delighted that at last he has a chance of giving everything he's got. With his first shot he shattered my lamp. I took refuge under the sofa, where, in relative safety, I can devote myself to my books. I am reading *Sindbad the Sailor*. It occurs to me, however, that this is not a text worthy of the times we are witnessing. I crawl to the shelves and pull out a slightly yellowed volume: *The Triumphant Progress of the Centrifugal Pump in Public Utilities*. Bullets clang against the springs of the sofa. The springs respond with a long vibrating note.

About noon the old man either exhausted his ammunition or went to see an eye specialist. My landlady came back with the news that the police had confiscated all the pictures of bearded men in photographers' windows. She could not explain why. She repaired my braces.

I could not get the puzzling news about the photographs out of my mind, and my recent reading about pumps had stimulated my enquiring spirit. I put on a false beard and went out. Two field policemen stopped me at the very first street corner. They took me to a photographer and took a picture of me, developed it and instantly confiscated it.

That night it was difficult to sleep because an armoured car was patrolling on our roof and checking the documents of the cats which always prowl there. I was told that only one cat had his papers on him but he too was arrested. After all, an ordinary cat carrying authentic personal documents is enough to arouse justified suspicion.

My neighbour went out today wearing a green polka-dot dress.

Since this morning thirty men have been working on the shiny dome of the Town Hall and painting it black. That dome used to shimmer even on cloudy days, but a siege is a siege. As I was watching, one of the painters slipped and fell to the pavement. He broke his leg. As they were lifting him, he shouted: "For the Fatherland!" On hearing this a citizen passing by grabbed a stick from another man and broke his own leg. "I also want to make my sacrifice!" he shouted. "I'll do my bit!" These cries excited him even more and for good measure he also broke his glasses.

In the circus, from today, they will be showing only patriotic numbers, and not all of them at that.

The family of our caretaker is showing signs symptomatic of the food difficulties in a besieged city. On coming home I passed the open window of their basement and heard the caretaker say to his little son: "If you don't behave I'll eat your dinner." His voice was full of ill-disguised covetousness.

I shrugged my shoulders. Why shouldn't a father admit frankly that he is hungry. Surely, the child would understand. I was indignant at this hypocrisy.

The landlady greeted me with another piece of news.

"Do you know," she said, "that there will be no Christmas this year? All the Christmas trees are to be sent to the barricades!"

"Oh, don't you worry about Christmas trees," I interrupted. "You'll hang your decorations on the asparagus fern."

"On the asparagus! Holy Mother," she wailed. "Nobody has ever done a thing like that!"

"My dear lady, better on the asparagus than on nothing at all."

She reflected over my words.

"Yes, you are right," she admitted, "but what if they take all the asparagus to the barricades, too?"

I had no answer to that one.

In the streets messenger-dachshunds are running about. Clearly something has happened.

The first meeting of the General Staff: it is reported that there was a difference of views on the possible use of the cannon outside the Town Hall. There is general agreement that the cannon should be fired at the enemy but some want to do it on a State holiday, others on a Church holiday. There is also a group of the centre which recommends as the best solution that a new State holiday should be proclaimed on a day which also happens to be a Church holiday. The left has immediately split into two groups; one which wishes to consider the motion proposed by the centre, the other regarding the proposal as wholly opportunist. Soon the extreme left splintered still further, with one group demanding the passing of a condemnatory resolution, while the other recommended that general reservations should be formulated in a non-committal form, primarily for internal reasons. A similar division also developed within the wing that wanted the cannon fired on a Church holiday and different groups within it have adopted different attitudes to the proposal from the centre.

In the afternoon my braces broke once more. I was ashamed to ask my landlady to repair them again. After all the woman has some right to a private life. So I stayed at home and made notes from "The Triumphant Progress".

In the evening I felt tired. After my intensive intellectual labours I needed some distraction. The darkness in the street (the man responsible for lighting the lamps was still in hospital) emboldened me; nobody could see that my braces were torn. I slipped into a bar where I met a nice man. He turned out to be the gunner responsible for our cannon. He confesses that he had no idea how to fire it; his real occupation was growing silk worms and he had been assigned to the cannon because of a clerical error. I had to hold up my trousers with my left hand while raising my glass with the right.

Time passed quickly. Soon we were friends and we were embracing each other. Alas, I couldn't embrace him with both arms and I was afraid that he would think of me as a cold, stand-offish and reserved person. On my way back I had to crawl along the walls because the old short-sighted man had obtained some more ammunition and bullets were whistling along the street.

The landlady had bolted the door from the inside. Undecided what to do I went into the garden and looked into the windows. Some people's lights were still on, among them my neighbour's. I saw her. She was so scantily dressed that she was shivering from the cold. I nearly cried out of compassion. How can one be so careless about one's health?

As I had gone to bed late, I slept till noon. When I got up I heard the important news. There had been a second meeting of the General Staff, and the centre group started splitting because of the different views adopted by its members on the positions taken by the groups of the left and the extreme left and the three groups of the right. The next item of news concerned the Town Hall. A ceremony had taken place there during which our old man, in recognition of his voluntary and vigilant fight against the enemy, was awarded a decoration and given a new rifle with a telescopic sight. I ran straight to the chemist and bought some bandages and iodine. I shall always have them with me. I heard also that the ceremony had not passed without a scandal. Because of his short sight the old boy had pinned his decoration upside down. When his attention was drawn to it, he replied with bullets and, shouting that he would not allow a single enemy to escape, he ran out into the streets. His decoration strengthened his readiness to sacrifice. What nobility! What zeal!

Life in the city tires me. I feel that it is time to make an excursion, to lie somewhere on the grass, with only clouds above my head. Will the weather hold? There are so many beautiful cathedrals and monuments in my city. The seasons change so miraculously, as if nature wished to give us a permanent spectacle with a subtly changing décor. I am sure that if one went to the outer fortifications and climbed a wall, one could look southwards and see an unlimited world. Is there anything lovelier than to stand on the seashore at five o'clock on a summer morning, to stand by the sea on which we shall soon sail southwards and southwards? I am sure there is, and this very certainty makes us hop gaily and wander farther and farther. Of course, these were only my thoughts. I was gravely handicapped by the absence of serviceable braces. My ignorance of practical matters prevented me from finding a remedy, and a feeling of shame did not allow me to seek help. In any case every minute brought new developments. An official communiqué announced that the cannon would be fired at the enemy the following day.

Preparations for the event were most elaborate. According to official orders everybody had to find a helmet for himself. This helmet could be worn during the rest of the siege, but it was compulsory on the Day of the Firing. The orders caused a great deal of confusion. My landlady got busy with her scissors, needle and thread and then entered my room wearing a helmet made of felt taken from her old school hat which, having spent half a century in the loft, smelled strongly of moth balls.

"Is that all right?" she asked uncertainly, as if ashamed of something.

I was surprised. Contrary to her normal custom she had done all the work in silence, without the loud grumbles and complaints she always voiced when complying with any official instructions. Thus I had had no warning.

"Fine," I said. "Most becoming. It makes you look young. But, you know, perhaps it isn't quite stiff enough. A helmet should be hard."

"Oh, what shall I do?" She was distressed. "I've darned it as well as I could."

"It isn't that," I tried to explain gently. "You know, it's just in case. Anyway, you must have a piece of sheet-metal somewhere, a baking tin or even an old unwanted kettle. . . ."

As far as I was concerned the solution of the helmet problem was simple. As soon as my landlady left my room I threw out the asparagus fern and put the pot on my head. This did not afford me much protection, even from splinters, but I was not worried. All I wanted was to avoid trouble with any police inspection. Just for one moment I was not entirely happy with the thought that we may really need the fern for Christmas.

171

In the evening, after a day filled with preparations, I decided to seek some relaxation by taking a walk in the cemetery. I found there what I wanted: peace and silence, so soothing after the streets filled with excited crowds, most of them already wearing helmets. Everybody was in a hurry to complete his shopping before the holiday when everything would be closed. Walking slowly along a path I came to an unfinished obelisk marking the official grave of the two goldfish, which were killed on the first day of the siege. Out of habit I am referring to the "goldfish" though this description does not tally with what is written on the tombstone.

To my surprise I met my neighbour, who, like me, must have slipped out of the hubbub and confusion in search of some peace. A lock of her hair had escaped from under a small helmet made of corrugated tin. I felt bashful.

"How quiet it is," I said, standing in front of her.

"Yes, very quiet," she agreed.

"They will fire the cannon tomorrow."

"So I hear."

She took out her mirror and adjusted the helmet.

The firing of the cannon was not successful. My landlady reported this to me. There was no official communiqué. I thought that the gunner I had met must have told me the truth, but I also heard that the failure was not his fault. Possibly there were other reasons. In any case there was a great deal of talk about it. Later I was preoccupied with other matters because I wanted to make my excursion to the walls. As you know, at that time I did not go out much because of my braces. I lied to my landlady and told her that my feet hurt and I had too much work at home. To reinforce my point I showed her the open volume on *The Triumphant Progress of the Centrifugal Pump in Public Utilities* and my notes on it. As for my excursion, I counted on the fact that in the outskirts

172

there would be hardly anyone about, especially that I was planning to set out in the late afternoon. I spent the rest of the Day of the Firing at home, planning my excursion and dreaming about it. Having switched off the light, I stood for a long time by my window.

When I woke up the next day I heard my landlady crying in the kitchen. As I lay in bed I wondered what could have upset her. At last she brought my breakfast, the newspaper and the sandwiches I had ordered for my excursion. She left them all on the table and fled in tears. My photograph was on the front page of the paper and with it an announcement that the person responsible for everything has been and is—me.

I was less surprised by it than I expected. After all, how can one be absolutely sure that one is not responsible for everything? I stayed indoors, glad for once that the broken braces compelled me to do so. I would not have liked to show my face to other people if it was all my fault and they were convinced of it.

It was a pity that the pleasure of my excursion should have been marred. When at last I left the house, one of my hands was holding up my trousers, with the other I shook the caretaker's hand. I gave all my books, including *Sindbad the Sailor* and *The Triumphant Progress of the Centrifugal Pump in Public Utilities* to my landlady. She asked me to write to her from time to time.

I was glad that dusk was already gathering. The man who used to light the lamps had not yet recovered. I went down into the yard hoping to catch a glimpse of my neighbour through the window. I did not see her, but I heard her talking to someone. I recognised the voice of my friend, the gunner.

I made off in a southerly direction. I did love my city. Its walls exuded the gentle, deep warmth that stones give up at the end of a sunny day. I have always admired true architecture, everything that is wise and simple, that follows naturally, everything that is great and beautiful because it owes its existence to a reflex of nature. That is why I enjoy living, when it is possible.

I had thought of going to the old citadel which has long been deserted. I was walking towards its ancient but still tall walls on which high green grass was waiting to be cut. I had left behind me the noise of the streets and was making my way between the deserted bastions which age had given the shape of round humps. All their military meaning had deserted them, leaving idyllic mounds that still carried a slight aura of uneasiness.

I was glad that my excursion was going according to plan. I had hardly met a soul and I could, without embarrassment, hold up my trousers with one hand, while carrying the sandwiches in the other.

Feeling somewhat tired by my rapid march I sat down for a while in the valley between two high parallel walls which were stretching into the distance. I had followed the bottom of this defile for quite a time and now, in the deepening dusk, I could only see a strip of the aquamarine sky. Staring at that sky I noticed a sharply defined silhouette of a man cleaning a rifle. On his chest glittered the disc of a medal.

Of course it was the old man with conjunctivitis, so intent on chasing the enemy. His devoted voluntary service must have taken him to the outskirts where he was now holding guard. Though full of admiration for his persistent devotion, I was nevertheless afraid that however good his intentions may be, a mistake on his part could not be ruled out.

Fortunately he did not notice me. Trying to make no noise, I resumed my walk along the defile. Soon I left him behind. I could have moved much faster were it not for my falling trousers which I had to hold up all the time. If only I had some serviceable braces! Those silly inhibitions did not desert me even there. I was alone. There was no one to embarrass me.

Then, after all, he fired. Lying on the grass with my face touching the earth, I felt in my heart a pain, a blunt, dull, stupid pain.